BORN AT NIGHT

BORN AT NIGHT

A VAMPIRE LEGEND

Nicki North

Nicki North
201 Kimberlee Court
Bonduel, WI/54107
www.nickinorth.com

Publisher's Note: This is a work of fiction. Names, characters, places, and incidents are a product of the author's imagination. Locales and public names are sometimes used for atmospheric purposes. Any resemblance to actual people, living or dead, or to businesses, companies, events, institutions, or locales is completely coincidental.

Book Layout ©2013 BookDesignTemplates.com

Born at Night/ Nicki North. -- 1st ed.
ISBN 978-0-9973677-0-6

*To my main vamps: Stefano, Jim, Dmitri, and Oliver.
Without you, this weird story
never would have happened. Thanks.*

*Once upon a midnight dreary, while I pondered,
weak and weary...*

—EDGAR ALLAN POE "The Raven"

Chapter One

I AWOKE ON A NIGHT LIKE ANY OTHER. Except it wasn't. Because that's just it. It was night. The sun had gone down and I felt this incredible hunger—or rather thirst—which put me on the edge of frenzy. Something was different; I could feel it. Something was very wrong.

I still remember this night as though it had happened yesterday, not three decades ago. But prior to that night, that first moment of Awakening, the day is blank. My entire past is blank. Gone. Erased. A true tabula rasa.

So I'll start at the very beginning of what I do remember. Wakefulness. My sense of awareness returning to me. My eyes remained unopened, each lid an anchor of sleep, weighing down like I had been sedated. The strange tingle of consciousness slowly crept through my frame, becoming more alert with each agonizing second.

It was at that moment when I realized I couldn't hear my heartbeat; I wasn't breathing. A tumultuous terror exploded, enveloping me in a heavy blanket of fear. A crippling dread came over and tucked me in. But still... no heartbeat, no sweat, no breath.

Was I dead? Whatever it was, I felt a desperate desire to die. To be rendered insensible.

And then I felt the hunger. It took over any other sensation as my eyes snapped open and I jolted upright, screaming from famish.

"Hello."

The voice came from behind me and echoed off the barren walls. The room I found myself in was foreign to me, or so I thought. I didn't know if I had been there before, I couldn't remember anything from before a few moments ago.

Not knowing what else to do, I slowly swiveled around to face the source of the voice. I kept expecting to hear my heart pounding against my chest to accompany the flood of terror that was rushing through me, but still, there was nothing. As my eyes finally met those of the voice, they locked in place. I couldn't tear them away, no matter how badly I wanted to. I was paralyzed. Not physically, but paralyzed by fear.

The man standing in front of me could not have been a man, could not have been human. He was tall, garbed in a pair of tweed pants and a ragged frock coat. But this was unimportant. It was his face that enraptured and terrified me, turning my whole world upside down.

Velum skin stretched over a gaunt face that was covered by long black hair. Slightly pointed ears poked out from underneath his veil of hair and piercing yellow-green eyes studied me. There were no whites to those eyes, just electric yellow interrupted by vertical pupils. Cat eyes.

His head tilted in what seemed like amusement and he smiled at me. It was a smile I have never forgotten and one that I never will. As his thin, chapped lips slowly and deliberately curled upward, they revealed a set of yellowed teeth and a pair of fangs. Fangs that were dribbled with blood.

"What do you remember?"

His voice was deep, but not too deep, more like that of a tenor. And it was coarse, making me think of sand-paper, slowly grating against skin. It sent a tiny shiver down my spine, but at the same time, I found what seemed to be comfort in his sandpaper questions.

"I…" my voice came out sounding like a parched child, scared and begging for something to drink. I swallowed and said, "Nothing, I don't remember anything."

The strange man with the sandpaper voice gave a near imperceptible nod and said, "Do you remember your name, my Child?"

It should have occurred odd to me that this inhuman stranger had just addressed me as his child for reasons unknown, but the title didn't make me bat an eye. I wracked my brain, trying to recall my name, and the task almost made me forget about the gnawing hunger.

"Maaria," I said at last. "My name is Maaria."

"Now it is Maaria Naeva. Maaria, Born at Night."

He motioned toward the window and I looked outside. Over the roofs of the empty shops and the quiet apartments above them, the light of the slim crescent moon illuminated everything. I saw details, which—before that night—I had never been able to see in daylight. The small cracks in the mortar of the brick buildings, the glistening petals of the floral wallpaper in a dark apartment window. Something about it brought a pervading sense of unease, but again, there was some sort of a strange comfort in it.

And then the hunger was back. With a mind of its own, my hand grasped my stomach, completely out of habit, my human reflexes.

The man looked at me with the same look of amusement, like he knew something I didn't. And he did. At that moment, I still hadn't grasped the reality of what had happened, hadn't even the slightest clue. I was disoriented and afraid, but still at ease. Something was clearly wrong here, but it felt all right. It felt normal.

"You're hungry? Come," he said as he held out his hand to me, "drink."

A look of confusion must have been etched on my face, because his lips curled into a smile. I looked at him tentatively, eyes shifting between his open hand and the cat eyes, which somehow managed to convey a look of trust.

I searched for words, but only stammered, "I don't…" My voice trailed off into confused silence. And when my words faltered, I watched the path his hand took—up to his mouth, with lips still curled tightly against spoiled milk teeth.

And then time stopped.

I watched as he pressed his wrist against one of those yellowed fangs and punctured the skin. Barely, but enough to draw blood. And as I watched that first drop of vermillion blood trickle out and curl delicately around the curve of his finger, my hunger came back in violent pangs.

My eyes widened with desire. With need.

And he looked into my lustful eyes and said, "Drink."

Before the words even escaped his lips, I was there, kneeling before him, lips wrapped tightly around his wrist, sucking his blood from the puncture.

As I drank, the cloying metallic flavor of blood coated my tongue. Where I expected bitterness, it tasted almost sweet. I had been gorged on emptiness and suddenly this blood became the only thing that could fill me. Madness was creeping in. Tendrils of hysteria wriggled into my psyche. I was euphoric, frenzied, on the verge of losing myself to this seemingly un-quenchable thirst.

And then as quickly as it came, it was gone.

The man ripped his hand away from me and immediately, the maddening desire vanished.

"That's enough for now," he said, pulling the sleeve of his coat down.

He paused, looking down at me with an indecipherable look in his eyes. And then his lips parted slower than any pair of lips ever had before, and in a low voice he said, "Do you know what I am?"

It wasn't until he asked the question that I had given it any thought. But I knew what he was, what he had to be. I just couldn't belief it.

"…A vampire?" I nearly choked on the words.

He nodded in that nearly imperceptible way again, and I suddenly recognized the look on his face. It was apologetic.

"Do you know what you are?" he said.

An icy cold horror shook my bones. I knew it, deep down, but his question forced me to face the reality of it, to acknowledge it, to say it aloud. I built up my courage and it finally came out as a faint whisper.

"A vampire."

I swallowed down the dread.

"Yes, Maaria Naeva," he confirmed in sweet sandpaper tones, "you are a vampire. I am your Sire and you are my Child." He paused, licked his chapped lips. "You remember nothing from before you Awakened?"

"N…no. Nothing." I shook my head.

A faint sigh escaped him.

"I have been watching you, to make certain you were the one for me to sire. You were an artist, a writer. But you were struggling. Poor, without work. You fell into a depression. You were a drug addict, Maaria Naeva. Heroin."

He paused and his eyes bore into me until I looked right back into them. And he said:

"This is your second chance.

Chapter Two

M Y AWAKENING HAD PRESENTED A new beginning to me. The night after my Sire left me, I stole a car from a vacant park and ride. It was something I never thought I would do, but as it turns out, being dead drives you to do a lot of things you never thought you would do. So I took the car and drove off into the midnight, searching for a new place to call home.

After a few days I found myself in a small town not far from Milwaukee. It was a wealthy neighborhood whose population was ideal for someone like me. Small enough that the nightlife was fairly dull and I didn't have to worry about many mortals ambling around after dark. And large enough that everyone minded their own business and I could get away with the thing that every vampire needs to get away with—feeding. It was the perfect place.

Not far out of town, next to the charred remains of a burned down farmhouse, I would find the abandoned shed I would call home for the next month.

As a vampire, with nowhere to really be but out of sight, one might think a month is quite a short length of time to stay in one area. And it is. But that story will explain itself in due time.

This little shed didn't look like much, but I didn't exactly have a memory of a home anyway. Of course I saw the other homes around me in all their extravagance, and knew that an abandoned shed was not much of a home at all, but these things didn't matter to me anymore. My shed was a ten-by-ten room with a single window and a wooden door with no handle. Everything was wood. The floor, the walls. And the hundred square-foot space inside was completely empty. In a human attempt to make this place seem homier, I found my inspiration in a dream. My first experience having a daymare.

My eyelids fluttered and struggled to open. When the light finally flooded in, I was consumed by the confusion in my surroundings. Everything was blurred and dizzy. I was conscious, but my awareness was next to none.

A nausea crept over me and bile rose up in my throat, burning. My gaze shifted down and I found myself lying in an empty and dirtied bathtub. An unprecedented groan escaped my lips, startling me, and next to me I saw the blurred shape of a spoon and a needle sticking out from my arm.

A lump formed in my throat and I tried to swallow it down with the bile, burning again. The salty sting of tears rolled down my cheeks. The dizziness worsened, coming in waves now. Doubling and doubling. And then everything went static. White noise rang in my ears. I looked out the bathroom door. A million miles away, I saw a mattress. A little desk with a lamp.

I sputtered and choked, foam spewing out of my mouth. Drenched in sweat, my wet clothes clung to my hollow frame. My heart thumped in my chest, threatening to burst through my ribs, and the sound of its efforts reverberated off every inch of my skull, drowning out any other sound, any other sensation.

My body shook. Convulsed. I was struggling to breathe, panicking, trapped inside myself like a virtual reality hell.

With a gasp filled with phlegm and bile, my eyes floated over a window that watched over the mattress. The last thing I saw before my eyes rolled into the back of my head was a pair of yellow-green eyes peering through the glass.

Perhaps it had been Mornor—the name my Sire shared with me. Then again, perhaps it was just the works of a delusional mind that was overdosed and clinging desperately to its last thread of life.

Whatever the case, I knew this dream had been a memory. My final moments as a mortal. The last minutes before Mornor would Awaken me, giving me a new life, a new purpose, a new cause. A second chance.

I didn't know then what this cause would be, and I don't think anything could have prepared me for what this new life would entail, but I was so certain this new chance at life gave me purpose. It had to. Because if it didn't, Mornor would have just left me to die.

It was my fourth night in this new town and when the moon rose and I awoke, I looked around my little shed with a touch of pride. I slept on a twin mattress covered by an old, unwanted quilt I had found in a dumpster. Coffins were not required. On the opposite side of the room sat a desk I found inside the farmhouse with a little reading lamp on top. And on the wall next to it hung a mirror.

I walked over to it and gave a smile.

Staring back at me was the same heart-shaped face, framed by a short asymmetrical bob of black hair, with now slightly pointed ears poking out from beneath. A small nose, eyes that no longer had any whites, just a yellow-green hue punctuated by vertical pupils, and a pair of full lips that parted, showing off fangs that glittered faintly in the moonlight.

A memory came pouring in—the first time I had seen my reflection since my Awakening.

It was my second night of unlife and Mornor and I were walking down an alley. We turned onto the main street of the little village and in the dark shop window, I caught sight of my reflection and jumped a little. Not by my new appearance, but by the simple fact that there was an appearance at all.

Mornor must have understood this because he chuckled softly, which sounded more like a purr than anything. He stopped and turned back toward me, his sandpaper voice trickling into my ears.

"Did you really believe you could no longer see your reflection, my sweet Maaria?"

He was teasing me.

"You've got to warn me about these things," I said. "I don't know what vampire lore is true or not."

"Mortals got most everything wrong about us, you see," he said. A small smirk crossed his face.

"What did they get right?"

"Sunlight. Fire. A stake to the heart, though this will only put us in a coma. To kill us, you need to drive the stake through the heart and then either burn us or

behead us. Garlic, crucifixes, coffins, the rest is all…well, quite a load of shit. Preposterous, really."

He spun forward and arched his arm so gracefully through the air, beckoning me to follow.

During the week I had spent with Mornor, his disposition of tenseness quickly faded. His subtle sense of despair was replaced by humor and an aura of eagerness. As I became more and more acclimated to unlife, he became more and more keen to show me the gifts of vampirism, rather than the obvious curse of it. He had a voracious appetite for adventure, telling me more times than I could count that if a vampire could not romp and adventure, could not engage in all the things one couldn't while mortal, then there was no point to being a vampire at all. That he would rather have rotted in the ground like the rest.

He told me to let go of everything tying me to my mortal life.

'It will do you no good, Maaria Naeva. It will only bring forth a despondency that will result in nothing but a pile of ash.'

And how could I not have trusted him, with that comforting sandpaper voice? How could I question him when he told me to live with reckless abandon, that it was the only way to survive?

And though part of me always held the nagging suspicion that this unlife called for caution, I would, in time, learn otherwise.

I stepped away from the mirror now. I had on what I wore as I died. A loose black t-shirt and a pair of blue jeans, holes in the knees. I grabbed the hooded sweatshirt I had stolen and pulled it over my head, making sure the hood cast a shadow enough to conceal my eyes.

Opening the door of my shed, I took my first steps out onto the moonlit earth. The night was beautiful and full of promise. And this is where my story really begins.

Chapter Three

IT WAS A TUESDAY. I REMEMBER THIS BE-cause at the time, I had not yet lost my mortal habit of keeping track of the days. I walked along the outskirts of town in hopes of finding a mortal to feed from. When it was clear no one was lurking about, I headed further out yet, settling for a deer or some other wildlife.

When it comes to the feeding habits of vampires, we aren't limited to mortals, as some might think. We can feed from anything with blood pumping through its veins. Animals are quite obviously the least satisfying, but they do just fine. Humans are preferred. And it isn't necessary to drink them dry of every last drop of blood like some myths seem to say. Just a small drink is needed. A pint or so.

We don't need to worry about them running off and blabbering about the monster that sucked their blood out of their neck, either. Our bite is like a drug to them. Everything becomes a vague haze of pleasantness. If I didn't know any better, I would say a vampire's bite is a bit like heroin. So it's quite ironic for me, you see, because I've progressed from being the addict to acting the part of the dealer.

We can feed from other Awakened as well, which is clearly the most gratifying source of blood, but also the most dangerous. It's a difficult thing to manage, particularly if you're not invited to do so. You also run the risk of addiction—nothing ever satisfying your thirst again, save for the blood of a vampire. Our bite might be like a drug to mortals, but vampire blood is like a drug for us. It is the most seductive, most positively bewitching of all substances. And it isn't some drug you can buy on any street corner. Those who become addicted to vampire blood should prepare to suffer.

Funnily enough, the first taste of blood I ever drank came from the cold veins of my Sire. He was smart enough to never let it happen again, but insisted it was a necessary risk in order for me to truly and fully experience the transformation process of entering into this new life.

And I believe he was right. No other drink of blood has ever amounted to that first one. The thirst I felt upon Awakening was unbearable, incomprehensible, and with that first taste of sweet metallic blood, everything was more intense, intricate. More alive. I was more aware than I had ever been in my mortal life. I might not have remembered that life, but I knew it to be true. Amnesia has nothing to do with feeling, with knowing. I don't have any memories of my mortal life, but I understand what this world entails. It's funny I can know all these things yet have no idea who I am. My own actions surprised me sometimes, caught me off guard. I was rediscovering who I was. But I knew I was more alive than ever before. It's ironic that it was in death that I found such clarity, such a joy of existence.

I saw an overwhelming and comprehensive whole. A distinct separation between all sensory input— seeing branches swaying gently against the midnight blue sky, hearing the delicate rustling of leaves, smelling the wafting smoke of a campfire, tasting the blood coating my tongue, feeling the soft breeze grazing my skin. Everything separate, but coming together in this beautiful whole. There's really no way to convey the feeling to someone who's never experienced it firsthand. But that is what I experienced in this new life and it is what I experienced that

Tuesday night as I walked down the empty streets, in search of my next source of this shattering clarity.

I was near the very outskirts of town when I caught the musty scent of a deer.

When I say scent, I don't always mean exactly that. We can smell if and when we breathe, but it isn't a reflex anymore; breathing requires a conscious effort in unlife. So yes, we can actually smell things, but we can still smell without breathing too—scent is simply the only appropriate way to convey the sensation. Smelling without breathing is like a tingling sensation of another presence, an energy really.

I crouched in the grass and made my way into the trees. I felt vibrations in the earth below me as the deer, unsuspecting, walked right into my path. I tiptoed forward, positioning myself for attack.

I pounced. It snorted.

In the distance, screams. Screams which quickly faded into the whimpering of someone who knew it was the last scream their lungs would ever produce.

Before my feet had even touched the ground, I shifted direction out to the road. Up the street on the left was a church. A small, modest building. White wooden siding with the paint chipping off in liberal measure. Surely the people who attended liked to think they were humble, accepting and god-fearing people. They were the mothers with the What Would Jesus

Do? stickers on their cars, and full of fake, transparent smiles. They were the fathers who brought their guns to church to protect the rights their god had given them. The children who wore sweater vests and little floral dresses, indoctrinated and telling all their friends about the invisible man in the sky who loved them.

I crept through the treeline until the church was directly across from me. Peering through the tall grasses in the ditch I saw nothing. Pitch black. Total darkness. The moonlight that illuminated the American flag and inspirational message board outside was being absorbed by the windows like a black hole. I couldn't understand it. I should be able to see inside.

Another scream. This one shrill and guttural at the same time. Like a woman who screams when she feels a bug crawling up her arm, but when she turns to swat it away, realizes it's actually flesh-eating worms digging their way under her skin. A croaking voice travelled across the road. A single word echoing with the same astonishment I'm sure watch etched across the invisible stranger's face.

"Bitch!"

Hmm. Kind of a strange sentiment to be pronounced in an empty church, late on a Tuesday night.

Moonlight suddenly infiltrated the glass and I saw a mass of black fog looming inside. I heard quiet mutterings, but couldn't make out any words. The front doors swung open like a great wind had commanded them to do so and the black fog weaseled its way outside, briskly starting down the road in the direction I had come from. From behind, I could see the hidden form of a human being.

Curious and slightly uneasy, I crossed the street toward the church. My curiosity always seemed to get the best of me. Inside, I saw nothing out of the ordinary except for a lone pile of ash in the center of the aisle. An Awakened? But that must mean there are others in the area. The thought made me worried. I didn't think I was ready to be thrust into a world with other vampires just yet.

With a faint spasm of dread, I headed home, almost forgetting my thirst. It wasn't until I was nearly to the door when I realized my hood was down. How long had it been like this? Careless. What if someone had seen me, seen my exotic glowing eyes?

I shook my head. "I shouldn't let myself get spooked so easily."

"Boo."

I gasped. Tripped over my feet and stumbled backward into the wall, falling to the ground. This is not a good first impression. My eyes were wide as I searched for whoever said it.

"You shouldn't let yourself get spooked so easily," teased the voice.

I snapped my focus to the left, where it came from. The tall grasses in the field shifted slightly. Not as if the wind had blown them, but as if a chameleon had been hiding there, expertly blending into the foliage, and when it moved, the grasses appeared to shift. It wouldn't have been noticeable to a mortal, but to me it was plain as day. Or night, rather.

"Who are you?" I tried to mask the trembling in my voice.

"You can see me? Huh, impressive. It seems we're quite alike. You'd know it if you could see my eyes."

She had a voice that sounded like silver—light and pleasant. But there were also hints of a familiar sandpaper, a subtle grating that clung to the ends of her words.

"Who are you?" I asked again.

The grasses shifted again as she took a step forward and let her camouflage slowly dissipate.

She looked about my age, with golden brown hair fashioned into a loose braid that curled around her shoulder. Her skin was a warm olive color, but had that sickly and transparent wanness that only follows death. Her ears were proudly displayed, though the points were much less prominent than my own. And her eyes were just like mine. But instead of chartreuse, they were a cerulean blue.

We were alike. We were of the same race—the Myagoros. There are five races of vampires, each with their own unique characteristics and supernatural gifts. Nobody knows why or how or where we came from, but plenty have tried to come up with wild theories to answer all the big questions. I personally couldn't care less. I simply knew I existed and that was enough. I didn't care where I came from and had no desire to find out. This was, perhaps, very wise of me. Searching for those answers would lead nowhere, because anyone who was old enough to remember would be too mad to preach about it. That was, if there were even any vampires that old left.

"You're new?" the girl said.

"To the area," I said, pulling myself up from the ground.

"That's not what I'm asking. I know that much. Trust me, I take notice when someone new wanders into town." She stared at me. "How long ago were you Awakened?"

"Um…two weeks. Give or take."

It was stupid to be so honest. I had no idea whether she was friend or foe or whom I could trust with this kind of information, but I figured if she wanted to kill me she would have done it already.

"And you can see me? That really is impressive."
She paused, but her lips remained parted as if debating
whether to continue. "So," she said, "are you going to
invite your guest inside?"

"Umm…um…yeah. Come on in."

Stupid.

Inside, her eyes surveyed the walls before resting
on me once more.

"So you could see me. I'm assuming that was
inherited then. Your senses."

I nodded.

"You're lucky," she smiled.

"My Sire said the same thing. It's the only ability I
know, though."

"Mhm. What's your name?"

I didn't like the way she said it, like a challenge,
and I glared back at her.

"Maaria," I said at last. "Maaria Naeva. And you?"

For a fraction of a second her eyes widened and
anger flared through them, but then it was gone.

"Interesting name," she said. "I'm Sage Nyx.
Please, just call me Sage." The sandpapery end of her
sentence grated into the next.

Silence. You could cut the tension in the air with a
knife. I cleared my throat. "Well, it's uh…nice to meet
you."

"Do you have a phone?"

I cocked my head. "No, I—"

"It's 2012, everyone has a phone."

"I was told to get rid of everything tying me to my mortal life," I said.

That was the best answer I could think of. The truth. Looking back on it, I was not good at being a vampire. Not at the beginning. But it wouldn't be long before I grew quicker on my feet, would learn to lie on impulse, to control every physical reaction. I would eventually unlearn everything mortal life had taught me. Most of this would happen after this story, but that's because this introduction to my unlife had taught me so much.

"So...you don't have a phone?"

"I destroyed it," I said.

"Well get a new one then. You'll need it."

She walked over the desk and opened the drawer, taking out a pen.

"Why?" I asked.

She scribbled on the corner of the desk and said, "So I can get ahold of you. Why else?"

"What? We're suddenly friends now?" I asked.

"Text me when you get a new phone. Then erase the number." She tossed the pen to me and then turned away and waved, wiggling her fingers at me. "Au revoir, Maaria Naeva."

She opened the door and with her first step out, she disappeared. Not any chameleon camouflage, but completely invisible. I couldn't catch a glimpse of her.

I shut the door and leaned back against it, letting out a heavy sigh. Who was she? A member of my own race—her invisibility, feline eyes, and pointed ears gave that much away. But I knew no more than that.

And the way she said my name was full of spite. She spit out the word 'Naeva' like it was unworthy of being spoken aloud, like it had caused her physical pain just to say it. And I couldn't know if this was unusual or just the way she was, because I hadn't dealt with any Awakened aside from Mornor.

I tried to calm down, but the more I tried, the more I couldn't.

Had this Sage girl been at the church? She had to have been or how else could she have known where I was, where I lived?

I pushed myself away from the door and paced the length of the room. Each time I reached the wall and turned around, my thoughts changed direction.

Who was in that church? Turn. Were they even vampires? Turn. Am I safe here? Turn. What does Sage know about me? Turn. Should I leave? Turn.

The phone number scribbled on the corner of the desk stared at me, burning into my skin.

Why did she give me her number? Turn. Is she a friend? Turn. What about the things I saw at the church, are they friends? Turn. The black fog? Turn. Am I over-reacting? Turn. What would Mornor tell me to do?

Turn. Turn. Turn.

Everything was moving faster, becoming a dizzying blur as I started to panic. My hands gripped at my hair, pulling and stretching my scalp as I circled, circled, circled. I threw my hands down and shot through the door, lumbering outside like a parcel of drunken flesh on the verge of vomiting.

In a feeble attempt to regain my composure I mumbled, "I just need to get some fresh air."

Wow. How human.

Having a panic attack is a funny thing for a vampire. Not that it's humorous at all, but funny in the sense that it's quite peculiar. Imagine a panic attack without your heart pounding against your chest—that vital mech-anism of life screaming at you and threatening to burst right through your skin. A panic attack without the shortness of breath or the hyperventilating, unless you force that breath upon yourself.

You're left sitting there, mouth agape, looking like sort of mentally defective sociopath. No chest pain, no nausea, no sweat. Your body appears to be totally normal. No chills, no hot flashes, no numbness, no tingling. Nothing. Just inside your head, panicking, dizzy, and afraid. Depersonalization is at an all-time high because not only do you feel detached from yourself mentally, but physically as well.

It'd be pretty damn embarrassing for someone to find me in that condition. I can only imagine I looked like a drunk sorority girl stumbling out to where she'd regurgitate more Taco Bell and Fireball than anyone would like to envision. And regardless of my lack of necessity for breathing, it must have been the principle of the matter, because breathing that crisp air into my lungs cleared my head and calmed me down.

Then the thirst was back. I'd forgotten I hadn't fed all night. I looked up toward the moon, and judging from its position, I had few hours to go and feed. Being a weeknight, I figured my best chance at blood would be the alcoholics stumbling out of the bar right about now. And I needed the blood. Once the thirst began to gnaw at me, it's incessant, refusing to abate until my fangs sink into flesh.

THE THIRST OF A VAMPIRE IS DIFFICULT TO explain. It's not as though we're savages whose entire being is defined by some searing, white-hot lust for blood. It surely does define us—it underlies our every thought and action—but at this time, I truly thought there was a greater purpose, a reason for this unlife. This belief of mine does hold some truth. We can find purpose in unlife, but our purpose will always be ruled by the blood. It's inevitable.

But anyway, the thirst. It starts as a gentle tug at your consciousness. A stirring of the mind that one can only assume is caused by the carnal desire for regeneration. We're cold, dead bodies, still operating on some numinous substance that gives us existence without life. Life is in the blood. And that which we don't have becomes what we—by our very nature—desire. There is a lust, an aphrodisia, for it. As the thirst becomes stronger, we crave more and more the heat that resides in life. The supple motility and subtle stirring of life under the skin. And when satiated, there is this agonizing clarity, a complete submission to the senses that awakens what is dead in us.

Like the first drink of blood I had ever taken, there is a transcendence of the curse and an awakening to something that is beyond any human experience. Without blood, we are nothing.

I made sure my hood was up this time, and concealing my eyes and I headed off to the some shitty little dive bar. In the parking lot I heard a soft weeping. It was dimly lit so I figured this would be my best bet. Gravel crunched beneath my shoes as I walked toward a car, pretending like it was mine, and when I was near enough, I looked over acting like I was hearing the crying for the first time. Sitting on the back stoop was a man in a shabby business suit. His thinning hair accentuated his large ears and protruding forehead. He looked pathetic, sitting there sniffling between drags of his cigarette.

If I had remembered more of my mortal life, I'm sure I would have sympathized with this man, but I only remember that glimpse of my pathetic bathtub death. When it came to sympathy, I had none. I wasn't heartless, I just couldn't relate. I felt only faint echoes of emotions. And I had thought this was how all vampires felt, and how I would forever feel. How ignorant this was. Much sooner than I could know, I would rediscover sympathy. I would relearn what it meant to truly experience all those human emotions. Such a blessing and a curse to feel. To feel as this drunk and blubbering man felt.

"Hey, are you okay, my friend?" I asked.

"Bah, I'm fine. Iss jus' tough, ya know?"

"Yeah, I know, man. What's wrong?" I sat down and placed a gentle hand on his shoulder.

"Iss my wife," he blubbered, "she's gone!" He threw his arms up, his cigarette flying out his grasp.

Trying not to laugh, I said, "I'm so sorry. You'll be okay."

"I'm alone!" he wailed.

"No. No, you're not alone. Here, give me a hug."

I wrapped my arms around his bulging shoulders as he sputtered some sort of thanks under his beer-ridden breath. Thank god for alcohol. It made these mortals so complicit. With my head nestled on his shoulder, I bit and sunk my fangs into salty flesh and drank. He didn't move, didn't make a sound other than the continued weeping. It was that easy.

After I took my fill, I pulled back and he looked me with glazed eyes and a foolish smile. "Thanks," he said.

"No. Thank you."

I turned to walk away feeling satisfied. Not only because of the scarlet elixir I drank, but also because the man unwittingly let me slip the cellphone from his pocket. I was in a delightful mood. The exhilarating rush from feeding was reaching its peak. A sweet surge of adrenaline. The wind roared through my ears as I ran through the brush, each air molecule biting my skin. Not cold, necessarily, but a sharp whip of air that stung like cold did. What mortals would have seen as shadowed trees against a black sky, I saw as a juxtaposition between midnight blue and branches of birch. And as I ran past, the branches seemed to cling to each second just a little too long.

This was the freedom of vampirism—an autonomy that is never experienced in mortal life. I was given complete authority over my senses, a carte blanche. In mortality, you must play by a limited set of rules, but in immortality you are able to exist outside them. Immune to all order and inhibition.

And as I ran, the exhilaration burst through the apex of the mundane and into this inexplicable realm of all-encompassing alertness. A perception that was very much alive. This is what the night had become for me. I had been given the authority to play god. The night was ruled by the vampire and we could play it like a chess-board. No one had power over us. No one had power over me.

But as my shed came into view, I snapped back into reality. I was not the only vampire in the area. And I had to assume that I was a pawn among knights and kings. A daunting idea, but there could be no other truth. I couldn't help but feel, in that moment, that I was intruding, that I was walking into something I couldn't even begin to comprehend.

By the time I stepped inside, the sun was preparing for its rise above the horizon. I took the phone out from my pocket and punched in the ten digits that Sage left scribbled on the desk. I pressed enter and stared at the white screen, wondering what to say to her. It stared back at me impatiently and avoiding its blaring gaze, I licked my finger and rubbed off the marks from the desk. I felt it best to not let myself get on Sage's bad side.

Looking back at the screen, I simply typed:

Hey, it's Maaria.

Chapter Four

THE MOON HAD RISEN INTO THE SKY and I had awoken. A blinking green light caught my attention, flashing a few feet away. I grabbed the phone and stared at the notification reading: *1 New Message*. I closed my eyes, sighed, plucked up my courage, and opened the message.

Good evening Maaria. Let me take you out for breakfast.

I'd be lying if I said I wasn't a bit nervous, but I agreed to it and asked her where to meet.

Oh, don't worry. I'll come to you.

It made sense to meet here—she knew where I lived. But it was precisely this thought that worried me. I shouldn't be so trustworthy. I didn't know anything about her. I mean, how can you possibly trust someone who has an eternity to live and become more and more disconnected from humanity? How can you trust someone with no connections or ties, just looking for a way to amuse themselves for the remainder of their indefinite existence?

I shouldn't trust her. And so my thoughts morphed into this distrust and unfairness as I waited. I knew she was withholding information from me. Not that she had any reason to share it; she didn't have any reason to trust me either, I suppose. Still, a small panic churned in me.

Soon enough the door opened, but there was no one there. No one you could see.

I cleared my throat. "Sage?"

The vacant doorway responded, "Maaria." She said it in a way that implied a curt nod of acknowledgement.

Materializing with a smirk dancing on her face she said, "I hope you're hungry." Her smile widened and I couldn't help but return it. Nervousness gone. She turned around, waving her arm gracefully over her shoulder. "Come on."

She wore a beige trench coat with a drawstring hood and with our hoods up, we raced through the trees and romped through the open moonlight, only occasionally catching a glimpse of our eyes or the shimmer of moonbeams against fangs.

She ran as a ballerina danced—graceful and gentle—but with a ferocity. There was an animalistic quality only a vampire could give to something so innocent. Fascinated by her, I watched as she danced through the trees, her eyes harboring a sharpness that could cut through glass, even diamond. And it was then that she became something just short of magic in my eyes.

I had all but forgotten the wariness she stirred up in me, how uneasy she made me feel. And when we approached the edge of the trees, she turned back to me with a wild grin.

"You see those lights over there, down the hill?" she whispered.

I nodded.

"You know what it is?"

"No," I shook my head, my eyes not once breaking connection with hers. They captivated me. Two crystal clear pools of blue that seemed to oscillate as small ripples passed through them, never still.

"It's a university," she said. "Full of some of the most self-righteous mortals you'll ever see. Four thousand self-loathing Christian undergrads. All just sitting there, trapped in their little ten-by-ten rooms."

"I uh...I also live in a ten-by-ten room," I said.

She grinned. "Yet we have more freedom that they will ever know. They're the perfect candidates." She looked out toward the school, then back at me. "Shall we go show them the wrath of God?"

She didn't even need to ask. I flew past her. Then skidded to a halt. "Our eyes," I said. "What about our eyes?"

"Not to worry," she said holding up her hand. She wore a ring on her middle finger made out of silver with a black jewel jutting out from the center. The slightest grin crept on her lips as she turned the ring. And with a loud pop, the lights on the street lamps went out. "I know a few tricks."

And she ran. And I followed.

When we stepped foot on campus, she was no longer a savage ballerina, she was just savage. Hungry. Her eyes no longer spoke of enchanting fancies, but of the carnal urgency of gluttony.

I tugged my hood down further and we walked toward the front doors of one of the dormitories. Sage—who had apparently taken the liberty of stealing a student ID card—held it up to the sensor and admitted us into the building. The lobby was empty, but Sage turned the ring on her finger anyway, flickering off the lights. She stepped back and waved her arm in front of her, bowing a bit, as if to say 'lead the way.' I hesitated and my fingers twitched nervously.

"After you," she whispered.

This was my first time getting into some real mischief, pushing the limit on getting caught by mortals. It was thrilling. Gave me a sort of foolish courage. I headed down the hall toward the stairs, but spotted an elevator hidden to the left. I looked at Sage. A little grin trembled on her lips and we dashed to the elevator in unison. Inside, I pressed the button for the top floor and Sage turned her ring.

Black. So dark a mortal could never catch the slightest gleam of light from our eyes. But to us, this claustrophobic space seemed more alive, the tension nearly tangible. I could almost reach my hand out in front of me and touch the ache for blood.

Our third trip down the building, there were quiet footsteps from below. I pulled out my phone and turned on the flashlight, pointing it down toward the floor.

Ding.

The doors slid open and before us stood two boys, average height, average weight. But none of this mattered anymore. All that mattered was the life pumping through their veins like the ceremonial beating of a drum. Blood.

I saw Sage stiffen with desire as the scent wafted into the elevator.

"Light's burnt out in here," I mumbled as the boys stepped inside.

"Oh, weird." So unsuspecting. Sheer oblivion to the fact that two vampires stood next to them, waiting to suck their vital source of life from them. Two monsters invading the safety of their omnipresent god's school. It was deliciously evil.

The very instant I heard the soft thud of the doors closing, I turned off the light on my phone. Sage had already taken the boy on the right.

Before he even had time to turn around, she was tiptoed, one arm wrapped around his waist, the other caressing his jaw. The veins bulged in his neck as he struggled for a moment, but when her soft lips brushed against his neck in a delicate kiss, he instantly relaxed.

That was his mistake.

Sage's fangs sunk into his neck.

All this had happened in a few seconds and as the boy in front of me turned around in confusion, I pushed him against the wall and dug into his neck.

There was no romance in my act like there was in Sage's. I think I was too close to my humanity yet to toy with them too much. I hadn't fed from enough mortals to detach myself from them, to stop from thinking that I was one of them or they one of me. I had to remind myself they were here to feed from, that was it. I couldn't let myself get close to them. Couldn't let myself remember I was one of them just two weeks ago. It was still too much to think about, too difficult to comprehend.

Back on the first floor, the doors *dinged* open and we backed out, watching them sit there in a haze of pleasure and confusion. Eager to leave, I started toward the exit. Sage was still standing there, licking the blood from her lips. Once she twisted the ring and extinguished the lobby lights once more she followed.

And as we ran, Sage was no more a ballerina than she was human. It was the hunt that fueled her. Or so I thought.

When we got back to my shed, she spoke the first words since we arrived at the school.

"You've got style."

It sounded like a compliment, but the look in her eyes said otherwise. I grinned, hoping it would come off as genuine gratitude. Her coat flapped in the wind as she shut the door behind us, erasing the only source of distraction from the mounting tension in the room.

We stared at each other in silence.

"Why are you here?" she finally asked. "Why, of all places, are you here?"

She caught me off guard and my tongue stumbled around in my mouth, searching for an answer.

"It's not that hard of a question, Maaria."

That magic I found in her just an hour before? Yeah, it was gone now. Extinguished just as quickly as her demeanor had changed.

"Why the hell should I tell you?" I snapped. "Why should I trust you?"

"You shouldn't trust me. You shouldn't trust anyone. But if you want to live here with any shred of safety, then I suggest you answer the question. Soon enough others will know you're here, and for lack of a better word, *trust* me when I say they're not going to take it as well as I have. So. Why are you here?"

I chuckled. "You're taking this well? Really? Could've fooled me—"

"Why are you here."

I clenched my jaw. "I just drove. When my Sire left, I just drove and when I found myself here, it struck me as a decent place for a creature like me to live."

"You know your Sire?"

"Yes, I know my—"

"How long did he stay?"

"A week. Why?"

"What did he tell his sweet Child about this life? About being a vampire?"

"What does it matter to you? Why should I—"

"Damn it, Maaria," she snapped. Her eyes closed and she drew in a long breath. Opened her eyes. "Just tell me."

I tongued my cheek. "He told me to give up everything tying me to my mortal life."

"Did he," she said flatly. "Well, you've done a really great job at that. He must be so proud."

I scowled at her.

"Did he tell his sweet Child anything else?"

"You bitch," I said. "You don't even know him. Was he wrong in saying that? Was he wro—"

"Did I say that? No. What else did he tell you?" she snapped.

"This is my second chance."

She stared in silence for a moment before a harsh, metallic laugh escaped her. "Oh, that's rich. That is funny," she said. "Well, he picked a downright awful time to give you second chance. And you picked the worst region in the entire country to spend it in. Good job." She backed away and clapped slowly, mocking me with her jarring solitary applause. "Goodbye, Maaria Naeva," she said, spitting out the word again.

I glared and spit back her, "Goodbye, Sage Nyx."

Her eyes flashed with rage and then she turned and disappeared from sight completely.

ALONE IN MY SHED, I SAT AND PONDERED ALL the things I didn't understand. Sage had an energy that called to me, felt like a home. I mean, she was a bitch, sure, but it was unsettling the way a wave of her hand or ripple of light in her eye made me altogether forget about that. The two instances in which I'd seen this girl, she dragged uneasiness alongside. But then that glistening wonder in her eyes would make me forget it all.

I knew she was hiding things from me. It was undeniable that she knew other vampires in the area and what was going on between them. She talked of protecting me, but that couldn't be so. She was interrogating me, nothing more. Just using my naivety to her benefit. To get answers. About what, I couldn't know. She was as cryptic as the sky was black.

Sitting there, her magic no longer captivated me. Instead, there was an electric storm in my mind. Cluttered. I couldn't think straight, couldn't make sense of anything. Dark clouds rumbled and sparks of lightning erratically pierced through, confusing everything even more. This storm inside me made it hard to think or concentrate on anything other than the inconsistent strikes of lighting.

But it was in these moments of brief illumination that everything was slowly revealed.

A dance of debauchery.

Eyes swimming in a way I seemed to know.

An arm combing through the air.

A pair of lips spitting out my name.

Naeva. Naeva. Naeva.

A thin-lipped grin.

This is your second chance.

Mornor, my Sire.

My Sire. I thrust my body upward out from the chair. The walls a blur of swirling russet and burnt umber browns for a few dizzying seconds.

Her reckless fierceness, ridden with such grace. She moved in the same way as Mornor. Her eyes swam in the same fashion as his, with that devious gleam. The arch her arm followed through the air was the same that Mornor's arm had taken just over a week prior. Mornor's sandpaper voice even lingered on the ends of Sage's own words.

I felt a momentary comfort. In a world of darkness where I was completely alone, it now seemed I had some sort of connection.

But then that comfort was gone. There were more questions than answers. They flickered through my mind, but drowning them all was the lingering suspicion that Sage knew something I didn't, something she was deliberately hiding from me.

Anger flashed through me, followed by a creeping dread. Why? Why hide these things from me? To protect me?

I doubted it.

The dizziness was back. Sounds faded away into distant and booming echoes. The walls morphed into swirling browns again and I threw myself outside.

The air was different now. Dark clouds strolled across the sky with urgency. The air was electric. It set the leaves and branches in motion, biting the air with an acuteness that jolted me out of my anxious stupor.

As my clarity came back, so did a memory.

The room in which I had first Awakened to unlife. Mornor sat with legs crossed and leaned back into a chair with effortless cool. His elbow rested on his knee and he held his hand to his face, cracking his knuckles.

He gave a subtle grin. His yellow-green eyes pierced through his veil of black hair and right into my own pair of yellow-green eyes.

His sandpaper voice purred.

"You know, Maaria, every vampire is scary. But the scariest of them all? Yourself. I am my scariest vampire and you should be your own. You're thrust into this world so entirely and fundamentally different from the one you've lived your entire life. And if you want to survive, you must toss humanity to the curb.

*Bring the destruction of your humanity, your mortality.
Scare it out of you. Kill whatever parts of yourself you
need to. And then you must reconstruct yourself.
Rebuild."*

It was clear to me I hadn't listened to his advice. I
was a vampire who was afraid of being a vampire.
And all I could think was: You are a creature to be
feared. You've been given a second chance. And this
is what you do with it? Cower in fear? If you waste
your gift like this, you deserve to die.

And so I ran.

Across the street and into the woods, the sharp
wind roaring in my ears. The moonlight shone through
the gaps in the treetops, making them dance with a hint
of madness. The shadows became looming monuments
of darkness that seemed to be as three dimensional and
solid as the trees casting them.

I would hunt here, in the woods. And I would learn
from its wildness. The trees would teach me to
intimidate, and the snapping branches to instill fear.
The shadows would teach me to hide, and the golden
moonbeams about the seduction of lunacy.

And the animal I'd kill would teach me that I thrive
on that give and take. Here, I told myself, I would strip
away every bit of humanity, save for the human form I
possess.

I danced through the trees. Twigs beneath me snapped and crunched, creating a symphony of destruction. Its melody followed me; a steady pulse that did not falter or fail.

A bat flitted through the air above me and I heard its squeaks. I effortlessly traced the path of its flight through the darkened sky.

An owl called out with a mournful hooo and I heard the whoosh of air as it spread its wings and rose into the sky. I followed the delicate beat of its wings, living vicariously through the sound of his flight. The faint outline of the bird angled down through the trees and his claws hung threateningly beneath him, ready to grasp the phantom rustling on the ground. Frantic squeaks sounded and the bird pulled back up into the sky, with a mouse firmly in his talons' grasp.

I was completely absorbed in my surroundings, letting my instincts take over. But then it abated and I noticed an inconsistency in the melody of destruction my feet created.

I was no longer alone. Someone was following me. I changed direction, trying to throw them, but knowing full well it was most probably futile. Shadows began to shift; dancing to a song the trees did not. I stopped. Twisted myself around. Nothing. I bared my fangs. If I didn't know my pursuer, perhaps they didn't know me. Maybe I would seem a threat. But no one revealed themselves and the shadows now stood still. Unnaturally still. The tree branches swayed, but the shadows were concrete.

I turned and ran. Part in fear and part in knowing that if they wouldn't reveal themselves to me when they knew I was looking, I'd have to catch them off guard. The footsteps didn't follow this time. I peered over my shoulder and glimpsed a set of glowing yellow eyes. I stopped. Turned back to them. But the eyes had disappeared. With fangs exposed, I slowly stepped toward the spot where I'd seen them.

A faint outline exposed itself, the thinnest line of space where the pattern of bark on the trees didn't quite align. A Myagoros trick. If it hadn't been for the color of those eyes, I would have assumed it was Sage.

"Who are you?" I called out.

No response.

"Ohh, okay," I said, drawing out the words, being as sarcastic as I could.

And then I caught the subtlest motion in the stranger's disguise. I think I struck a nerve. So I turned and walked away, but nothing followed. Behind me, I heard a trickling of something dripping to the ground.

A physical haze of confusion struck me. Dizziness choked me and I couldn't think straight; everything was muddled. An echo of footsteps approached as if in slow motion as I struggled to maintain my balance.

The footsteps were still approaching when a solid face struck me and I fell to the ground.

Fangs. Inches from my face they thrashed, and above them was the blur of yellow eyes. I tried to thrust the things off me, but my arms were leaden. Hollow laughter echoed above me irregularly and I felt the biting sting on my cheek before I ever saw the hand strike me.

But with it, this stranger slapped a bit of my senses back into me. I pushed it off and saw a petite girl with a mess of stringy black hair. Those eyes were the only color in her—skin alabaster, draped in all black. A monochrome devil.

Not a second passed before a black fog covered her, leaving only her eyes unmasked.

I struggled with my body, fighting to get up, but she loomed over me with a small glass bottle in her hand. She plucked out the stopper and poured a pale red oil onto me. The moment it touched my skin, the confusion struck again, only exponentially worse.

Everything in slow motion once again. Her mouth opened, looking deformed and warped like the demon in a horror movie. Words jumbled out all broken and echoed against the walls of my skull.

"Don't worry… Maaria… I'm not here… to… hurt you… just put you… in your… place."

By the time the last words registered in my ears, she was already walking away and her reverberating laughter faded into silence.

And there I lay. Motionless, confused, and afraid.

I PUSHED MYSELF UPRIGHT AND RAN. THIS time, not with the abandon and ecstasy of my Awakened senses, but with a violent determination to kill. I don't know how much time had gone by as I waited for the effects of the oil to wear off, but as I lay there paralyzed and waiting, a senseless anger rose in me.

The deer didn't have time to know what hit him. When I saw him, I pounced and clung to him with a strength I didn't know I had. My fangs plunged into his neck and sucked until there was no more blood to drink. He made these awful sounds and I watched as his eyes clouded over with death.

And then I dropped him and traipsed off, drunk with the blood that was dripping from my chin and onto my shirt, splattered all over my jeans and trickling into my shoes. Rage made a messy eater out of me.

I reached my shed with less than an hour until sunrise. Sitting down on my makeshift bed, I felt satisfied that I had stripped away the remains of humanity. Or at least enough humanity to truly call myself a vampire—a being who thrived on death and lusted after life.

My shoulders shook as I cackled. I had forgotten all about the girl in the woods. This was my victory, who cared about some harmless fiend? Not me. Not then. My blood-caked jaw lifted into the air as my head fell back and I laughed with hellish hysteria. The colors in the room seemed brighter, the whisper of the wind louder, the fabric of the quilt softer, and the blood on my tongue sweeter.

I was immortal.

I had truly thought that I had been cured of my humanity, that killing a deer would somehow strip me of any mortal tendencies. But that was a gift unlife would never be so kind to grant me. And over the years I would lie to myself, I would ignore the truth. I would tell myself I was no longer human. But with age, with the passing of time, I would only feel humanity more keenly.

I may not have a mortality to remember, but humanity was carved into my soul and it will remain there forever.

During this short time, however, I was so, so sure my humanity was gone. But this was thirty years ago. I was naive then and I was young.

Chapter Five

DUSK. MY EYES SNAPPED OPEN. THERE IS no such thing as grogginess as a vampire. Waking up and falling asleep are as instant as the flip of a switch.

Outside, raindrops pattered against the roof.

I remember thinking, at the very beginning, how nature had it so easy. It didn't have to hunt for food, just wait for the sky to feed it. And then there was me. I had to sneak about, sucking the life force from mortals just to survive, to exist in secret. It wasn't very vampiric of me, but then again, I didn't make a very good vampire back then.

On this night, I thought instead, how nature seemed quite pathetic next to something like me. Nature can't take what it wants. It's forced to wait, starve, and possibly die, in the hopes that the sky will feel generous enough to nourish it. The plants and the trees and the grass, they have no power to do anything for themselves. Just slaves to the sky. But me. I get to feed from whomever I want, whenever I want. In a way, vampires are superior to nature.

I got out of bed and stood on my toes with my fingers laced together over my head, stretching my limbs. It felt good. I wanted to run, to hunt.

A pair of headlights streaked inside when I opened the door. I waited for the car to pass and stepped out into the cool rain, which showered onto my skin and rinsed the dried blood from my face and clothes. I lay down in the grass and looked up to the sky, raindrops pelting toward my face. I didn't close my eyes or even blink. This no longer bothered me like it would a mortal. What did it matter if my body was dead?

If I were still human, I would've found this lying down in the rain to be a peaceful experience. It would have brought a cleansing and renewing energy. Don't get me wrong, I felt the echoes of those emotions, but I ignored them. I pushed them away until I felt only the cool droplets dripping down my cool and lifeless flesh. Because, dammit, I was a vampire now and my humanity was gone.

These were such peculiar perceptions to have—knowing, yet never truly feeling. Did any vampire ever get used to them? They must. Surely Awakened who have survived for centuries must forget what it ever meant to be mortal, must not feel the silent echoes of humanity inside them, or remember what happiness or sadness is.

Perhaps they've forgotten the taste of peanut butter, or chocolate, or the smell of an onion. Maybe some don't even remember what an onion is, if they have isolated themselves from society for long enough.

I pulled myself up to my feet. My pants still looked like a Jackson Pollock painting, bloodstains decorating them all over. I needed a change of clothes. So I decided to go out and hunt, killing two birds with one stone.

Before I left, I ran inside and grabbed my phone. If Sage was going to play games, I would play them too.

Breakfast? My treat.

Of course, I had no intentions of hunting with her. I'd leave now, hunt on my own, and eventually she'd show up at my shed. And I'd be full, while she'd be hungry. And I would get what I wanted out of her. After all, I was a vampire, not a tree waiting for the rain.

I walked out the door. The thirst tugged at me. And following my feet rather than my head, I found myself heading toward the local campus—Concordia of Mequon.

The rain had reduced itself from a steady fall to a light drizzle and fog rolled in from the trees. These were perfect hunting conditions. I picked up speed and threw back my hood with a rush of confidence. The closer I got to campus, the thicker the fog got; right beside it was the coast of Lake Michigan.

Right around the last curve of the road before the campus entrance, I spotted a girl jogging through the haze. I crouched low and headed into the ditch, running quieter and faster than she could have moved even on her fastest day. She passed under a streetlight and the moment the shadows of early night enveloped her again, I attacked.

I snuck up behind her before she had time to know I was there, and tapped her on the shoulder.

She swiveled around and two saucers of fear stared back at me. And then I bit. The blood flowed out of her neck and into my throat. I dragged her into the ditch with me and drank until she was unconscious. I let her drop as the thrill of regeneration pumped through me. The immense flood of clarity came crashing in like waves.

I licked my lips. She tasted good; there was a hint of burning metal in her, the taste of fear.

Remembering I came here for clothes, I dropped to my knees and groped around her waist until I found the button of her jeans. I tugged them down, exposing the pink flesh of her legs and ripped them off her limp body.

She was still unconscious, but alive. I listened to her pounding heart, her ragged breath, sensed the subtle vibration of her pulse.

I pulled my own jeans off, still stained with dark blotches of blood. I tossed them onto the girl like you'd toss some moldy food into the trash and a soft groan escaped her as the wet denim slapped her skin. She would be one confused girl when she woke up.

I stepped into her jeans, struggling to tug the damp cloth up my legs, when I heard a vibration. My phone was still in the pocket of my jeans. I crouched over the girl and reached into the bloody jeans heaped over her. It was Sage.

I'm waiting.

"I SEE YOU FED WITHOUT ME."

Sage leaned against the door of my shed, waiting for me. Just as I assumed. A fire burned in her eyes and flickered dangerously as I gripped the plank of wood that served as a door handle and pushed past her. In a swift move, she twisted around and followed me inside.

She sat down on the desk chair, leaning her arm over the back and crossing her legs, staring at me expectantly.

I stared back at her dumbly.

"Why am I here, Maaria?"

"Mornor."

The slightest shake of her head and the furrow in her brows signaled confusion. Maybe I was wrong and she didn't know him. Maybe I had just been trying des-perately to justify my pusillanimity toward her.

"Mornor," I said again.

"Who?" she said, wearing the same confused ex-pression. But the feeble quiver that pealed out betrayed her.

"I think you know," I said softly.

"No, I don't."

"Mornor," I said again. "Mornor, Mornor, Mornor," I said it over and over, my voice amplifying with each repetition.

Sage's eyes ignited with rage and she bolted forward with a violent hiss. The thud of the chair being knocked to the ground was the only sound now. Like lightning, she was in my face and her hand gripped around my throat. Her fingernails dug into my skin and her upper lip curled up tightly, baring her fangs.

"Don't you dare speak his name! You don't deserve to be his Child, you pathetic leech." Spit flew from her mouth, splattering on my cheek.

My eyes filled with fear and hers with rage. Blood vessels swelled in them, the cerulean blue becoming a plum. I was locked in her grip. She was stronger than me, stronger than I had imagined her being.

She shoved me away and I stumbled backward. I wiped the spit from my face and laughed. "You're jealous of me, is that it? You're jealous of me? Why, because you're not his only Child anymore?"

She growled. "I never was his only Child. Just the only one still alive. They were all weak." She paused, hatred beaming from her to me. "Just like you. You shame him."

"And how is that?" I shouted. "Because I don't prance around the woods and keep petty little secrets like you do? Because I—"

"Because I actually listened to his advice!" The words started as a bellow and ended in a whisper. "I threw out humanity. I'm not trying to be anyone's friend. I help only when I get something in return, not out of some altruistic tendency. Some *human* tendency. So stop thinking I need to let you in on all my little secrets. I don't see anything you can offer me. So why should I tell you anything? To do you the favor of satisfying your meaningless curiosity? No, I don't think so."

"You owe me that," I said.

"Oh, I do?"

"We share the same Sire, Sage. And I left my home, headed out on a road to nowhere, and of all Awakened, I found you. *You*," I stressed. "That cannot be purely coincidence. You owe me this much."

She looked me up and down, calculating, as if this would somehow reveal to her whether I was worth a response.

After seemingly endless minutes, she heaved out a sigh. "What do you want to know?"

I thought about it. "Who are you?"

A long silence before she spoke.

"I was a part of the 1940s jazz scene in Chicago. A hipster with an opium addiction. I went up to Wisconsin to visit family, left my brother in the city. And sometime during my visit there, he found me, started watching me.

"I spent Christmas with my family, stayed there for New Years, and was planning to head back home soon. There was a show coming up—Sarah Vaughn— one of Ralph's favorites. He wanted me to be there for it." Her mouth lengthened in a sad smile. "We never got along with our family, never belonged there. We just had each other, Ralph and I. And then I went out one night, January 13th, 1945. And that was it. I never returned to Chicago, at least not to see my brother. I could never do that again. To him, to the rest of family, I had just vanished."

She shook her head, breaking free from her reverie. She looked embarrassed; she had been vulnerable and shared some intimate thing with me.

"Mornor stayed with me the same as he did with you," she said, "although he took the time to teach me a few tricks."

She smirked, at once redeeming herself and proving herself superior to me. It was an obvious trait to notice in her, but impossible to understand.

"And then he left. I've seen him once since, when I was back in Chicago with the Shrine. That was about twenty years ago."

"The Shrine?" I asked.

The corner of her lip curled up and she tilted her head like quizzical dog. "You don't know about our creeds? You really do—"

"I was alive and human up until two weeks ago. Don't patronize me."

"Fine," she said.

It seemed she derived some sick satisfaction from making me realize how ill-informed I was about our undead culture. But if it meant I would learn, I didn't care.

"The Shrine of Lilitu is one of our society's creeds. Some call it a coven, but it's not. You can find members anywhere; it's organized. Biblically speaking, the Shrine believes that Lilitu was the first woman created for Adam, not Eve. But she didn't want to lie beneath him; she wanted to be his equal. So she left the Garden and traveled out to the Red Sea. Angels were sent to retrieve her and bring her back to Adam, but she didn't want to go. So she bargained with them and they eventually allowed her to stay at the sea, but only as a witch, or a demon. Whatever you want to call it.

"Then years later, after Cain killed his brother, Abel, he was banished. And he found himself in the same place. Lilitu introduced herself, showed him the power that resides in the blood. Cue a passionate love affair, ridden with boundless evils. Blah blah blah. And she bore Cain's children. The first vampires. Half demon, half murderer."

"So what?" I asked. "It's like a religion for vampires?

Her eyes narrowed. "God, you really are useless."

I ignored her. "You said there's other vampires in the area."

"Yes."

"Okay, so I'm assuming not everyone gets along. You said this was the worst time for me to be here. What's going on?"

"That doesn't concern you."

"Yes, it does," I said.

She hissed and stepped forward.

"We're sisters, right?" I yelled.

"We share the same heritage. That doesn't make us sisters. We're vampires. We have no family and we have no home."

If I was being honest, I think I saw something like pain in her eyes.

"Why won't you help me," I asked softly. "Be a mentor to me, if we share the same heritage?"

"Because it means nothing to me."

"We're connected."

"We're not," she spit. "If you want my help, then prove yourself worthy of it. Simple as that."

"How?" I asked. "What makes me worthy?"

"Figure it out," she shrugged and walked out the door.

I watched her walk away, and then she vanished.

She didn't hate me. I knew that. If she had, she wouldn't have come over, wouldn't have told me any of the things she did. She knew as well as I did that we were connected, similar in some curious way.

The same bewitched substance that ran through her blood ran through my own. It ran through all of us, the crux of our existence; but ours—it flowed from the same specific source. Mornor. We were kindred undead.

And I would prove to her I was worthy. Of her help, advice, of being Awakened, if only to prove her wrong.

I walked outside and followed the footsteps Sage had made as she left. The moon was high in the sky, a watch guard over all the stars and the earth, granting me with a few more hours until sunrise. I pulled my hood up, tugged it over my eyes, and left my shed behind. In pursuit of something I didn't yet know.

I drudged along the same path I had taken only two nights prior, when everything was new, but normal, commonplace, unremarkable. Was it really only two short nights ago that I had thought I could find some normalcy here, in this strange place and new life? Two nights, but with a few minutes and miles I would discover anything but normal and unremarkable.

And that is precisely where my feet led me.

I gazed across the empty street and staring back at me was the faint decrepitness of the church. The church that uprooted the seeds that hadn't even had time to plant themselves firmly in the earth. The moon cast a light over it and allowed an expression of bored curiosity to peer right into my—perhaps absent—soul. I think it noticed this, knew what I was. Its inherent holiness saw my own unnaturalness. The silent acknow-ledgement passed between us without question, but still with an air of subtle disquietude.

An enmity welled up inside me. Something so simple as four wooden walls had suddenly made everything so complicated. Whether or not I was disconnecting from my humanity didn't matter right then, I only wanted simplicity. Monotony. Not to feel like a helpless pawn in a game filled with ancient kings.

A writhing shadow caught my eye. It wormed its way around the corner of the church for a fraction of a second until it vanished. A trick of the eye, maybe. No, that's a human thought. If I could distinguish each individual blade of grass sprouting from the dirt across the street, and the tiny veins in the grass beside me, that shadow was tangible and real, not some mirage.

I watched and waited until I spotted the tiniest tendril of shadow peer around the corner. It moved slowly and ethereally at first, but as it continued its sinuous journey it began to writhe and contort.

Moonlight refracted off a hidden something.

A flash of yellow.

I don't know if she felt me watching her or if she simply assumed I knew she was there, but she stepped around the corner and let her looming fog dissipate.

Fear struck me like a train. Blood dribbled from her chin, a wide grin spread across her face. If I still had a pulse, it would have quickened at the sight. She was terror in the flesh.

She stepped forward all slow-like and a whisper slithered across the street.

"If you've learned your lesson, I won't hurt you."

My eyes narrowed in distrust, but I didn't know where I could go without her following.

Another whisper tickled my ears.

"The bark is worse than the bite…Maaria."

She had uttered my name twice now and I had no idea how she could know it. And if I was learning anything from unlife, I knew there was only one way I could find out.

So I crossed the road.

Chapter Six

ORRY ABOUT THE BLOOD," SHE SAID wiping her chin. "I just had a snack."

Her voice spoke its own dialect. The vowels danced between intonations, creating recognizable, yet foreign sounds.

My eyes hardened and I slowed my encroaching steps. Wary of her, I asked, "How do you know my name?"

"I know a lot about you, Maaria. You can thank your friend Sage."

Anger shot through my eyes and she quickly added, "But don't worry, she didn't tell me about you. I read it all up here." Her jagged fingernail poked into the flesh of her temple. Blood filled the cracks in her lips as they curled upward.

"You read minds?" The words came out gingerly; I didn't want to push boundaries with her as I felt they were already bursting at the seams, ready to explode at any given moment. But I wanted answers.

She stepped forward and I glanced down at her combat boots. If her demeanor wasn't intimidating enough, her appearance surely was. Tattoos of strange symbols and runes marked her fingers and the side of her cheek, right along her ear. The bridge of her nose was rigid with some small scarification.

Her eyes followed mine until they locked with each other. Her chin stooped low in a small nod and she said, "You know what else I found up there?"

She didn't wait for an answer.

"She's jealous of you. You don't remember mortal life, but you can still feel it. Sage. She remembers everything, but can't feel it at all. The only part of life she still feels is the bonds of blood, of family. And right now, you're the only family she's got.

It explained why she shared her past with me, told me about the Shrine of Lilitu. Regardless of whatever issue she had with me, I was her family and she knew it, she felt it, somewhere deep down.

"She told that you came to the wrong place at the wrong time? She won't tell you why or mentor you because she's jealous."

"Why are you telling me this?" I asked. "How do I know you're not lying? How do I know I can trust you?"

A childlike giggle bubbled up through her throat. Such a sweet and innocent laugh from such a menacing body made my skin crawl. "Because I have no reason to lie," she said. "I have a certain contempt for Sage. She's prideful and arrogant without remorse. And I have a bone to pick with her."

I stared. "So you want to tell me the things she won't so I can, what? Hold it over her and you can get some sort of petty revenge?"

She scoffed. "You sound like you wouldn't expect that from a vampire. But yes, I need to get her attention."

I considered her offer. She might seem a little volatile, but the course of action was pretty damn clear.

"Only if you can tell me everything I want to know."

She replied with a smile. "Of course."

"Tell me your name," I said. My first demand.

We were sitting inside the church now. I, on a front row pew, and she, sitting cross-legged on the altar. In her hand she clutched a chalice filled with the remaining blood of her victim.

('You have to kill every now and again, Maaria. What's the point of taking without sometimes taking every last drop?' she explained.)

"You can call me Annabelle. It's my mortal name, not what I call myself now, but you don't need to know that name. What use would it be to you anyway? Names hold no meaning anymore. I'm just another monster."

I stared. She waited.

"Next question," she said.

Why," I said, "is it so horrible that I was Awakened now and that I chose this place to settle?"

Her grin widened at the opportunity to explain, showing off red-stained fangs. The hues of the stained glass window cast a shadow of red and violet over half her face that reeked of heinous phantasm. I shivered.

"We're a dying race." She paused and licked her lips. "There are less of us now than in any time for as long as any Awakened still alive can remember. But rumor has it, there's an object, long hidden, right here in this little white suburban town, that could change everything. Change history for the dead and living world alike if in the right hands. The single most powerful object in history that looms over every supernatural being like the threat of a swinging pendulum." Her finger swung from side to side. "And you've stumbled right into the middle of it."

"What's the artifact?"

She looked up at me and her eyes darkened. "The Ring of Solomon." Her voice hinted at either lust or hatred—I couldn't decipher which.

"Solomon. Like the Bible?"

"That's the one," Annabelle said.

"Here? Something like that here, in this little town?"

"Rumor has it."

"So you're telling me I've walked into some rumors, then? Doesn't sound very formidable."

Rage shot from her eyes. "The Primus wants it. The leader of the Nobilis Sanguis—sorry, I forget you don't know these things. Treacherous bastards. The Primus is old and delirious, but any member of the Royal Blood will listen to whatever spews out of his putrid mouth." She stood up and paced the length of the pews, chalice swinging gently in her grasp, blood circling the dull silver eternally. "So when this lunatic suddenly re-members that years ago, a member of some ancient lineage of Awakened—descended from one of the illegitimate sons of Solomon himself—came here with this ring that was stolen from Solomon millennia ago, and after carrying it from place to place, from Sire to Child, keeping it out of the hands of anyone and everyone—they believe it. And the Primus wants it." She took a swig of blood. "So it doesn't matter whether these wild claims of his are true or not.

We've got to assume they are. We've got to keep this ring away from him. He would end us." Her fingernail slashed across her neck and she made a strangled sound.

I stood up. "And what happens if you find it, then?"

"I destroy it," she said. "The Primus and the surviving members of the faction are the only ones who don't want it destroyed. I mean, other than this mysterious being who apparently brought it here in the first place. But it needs to go. We all know it. I know it, Sage knows it—"

"Why do you hate her? What do you two have against each other if you want the same thing?"

She smiled and glanced at the window. "That one will have to wait. The sun will be up soon. Besides," she said with a mischievous smirk, "I need you to help me dispose of this body."

Together, we carried the body out into the woods and dumped it into a dank ravine. The eyes of the practically embalmed corpse stared up at me blankly. Annabelle turned to me. "I trust you'll keep me informed about what you or Sage might learn about this ring. Considering you're going to tell her everything you know anyway. And I trust next time I see you, you'll have learned a few tricks."

She winked at me and her hand hurried down to twist a ring on her finger. Almost instantly, the black fog engulfed her.

"You're a member of the Shrine?"

The fog lowered to reveal her yellow eyes and she said, "Not quite."

And she ran off.

I AWOKE THE NEXT NIGHT FEELING MORE confused than ever. I didn't know how I was going to balance this crooked triangle that was Annabelle, Sage, and I. But knowing what was rumored to be happening wasn't enough. If I was going to play two sides of the same fight, I would need to know where their relationship lies.

I could assume they knew each other more than just in passing. Annabelle had said she had a bone to pick with Sage, so they must have some sort of a past together. Sage had never mentioned her, though. But should that surprise me?

Sage had said other Awakened wouldn't take kindly to me once they knew I was here, but I think last night had proved her wrong. Annabelle— unnerving as she was—had encouraged a relationship with her. Granted, it was only to serve her own purpose, but there was a certain kinship there. For now at least. Still, I would have to tread lightly.

Annabelle had been right when she said I would tell Sage everything I now knew, but before I did so, before I proved myself worthy, I wanted to know even more. I wanted to discover how much truth there could actually be in these rumors.

I knew there was a library close to the center of town, so I decided to go there. It would be closed now, but that meant so little to someone like me.

I grabbed my sweatshirt and phone and walked out the door. The grass was greener after the rain of last night. A vibrant energy radiated from the being-ness of the trees. I breathed in deeply, only to inhale the sick stench of worms that the rain had called up from the earth, and which permeated the post-precipitation air with a sickening thickness. I almost thought I was going to throw up.

If thinking the trees had a being-ness, thinking a deep breath of fresh air to be calming, and being disgusted by the smell of worms wasn't sign enough that I hadn't rid myself of humanity, I didn't know what was.

As I got nearer to town, there were more streetlights scattered on the roads. It was early in the night so I dodged them by trudging down alleyways whenever possible. I kept my head down so mortals would think I was only another delinquent trying to remain incons-picuous. Which wasn't entirely untrue.

I passed brick building after brick building, each more impressive than the last and I turned onto a road with a small gathering of neighborhood homes a few blocks down. On my left stood the library. I dashed across the street, taking extra caution to keep my hood over my face until I reached the pavement. Glancing up, the street signs read *Glenberg* and *Division*. I feigned waiting at the bus stop until all cars ceased to pass by and no pedestrians wandered the street, leisurely walking to some mundane destination.

I walked around the back of the building where I found a window that, for the most part, was hidden by some low-hanging branches. I pulled my sweatshirt over my head and wrapped it clumsily—and in retrospect, humanly—around my elbow. Biting my bottom lip and sucking in some air, I hoped no one would hear as I threw my elbow into the window with as much force as possible. Cracks spidered through the glass and with another blow, it shattered.

I climbed in through the pane and sped through the building until I found what I was looking for—computers. Sitting down, I opened up the browser and got to work.

While I'd been on my way there, I thought about what I should even begin to search for. Odd deaths, church records, past reverends, religious artifacts. Perhaps record of this ring wasn't even religious at all.

If there even was a record. But maybe it would have been thought to be some cult activity. It didn't matter. I had to try. Try to find something that could give me even the slightest chance of a lead.

1914. The Catholic parish German settlers built only 40 years ago was torn down after a severe decline in membership, and years later it was rebuilt, only to be struck by lightning and burnt down yet again, eight months later. Now, the church will be rebuilt a third time, with hopes of remaining far into the future. It will no longer be a Catholic Parish, but will instead be home to the first Lutheran church in the area...

LOCAL MAN MURDERED after townspeople presumed him guilty of murdering the Madam at local roadhouse and brothel. The madam was strangled and found in the bathtub. A disturbance was reported last night and officers found the contorted body of a man who had been purportedly thrown down the stairs. Suspects are still at large, please contact...

Local brothel and roadhouse on Murdock Road now closed down, purchased by local family who plans to turn the building into a farmhouse and call it their home...

Rev. Henry Loeber brings church attendance to new heights. Says he will continue to do so and looks forward to new and friendly faces. "The grace of God is boundless and it is quite remarkable seeing all these souls coming closer to Him and his bountiful mercy," says Lobber. He wants to introduce the idea of building a school...

1921. Only two short years after St. James Lutheran Church welcomed Reverend Christian Barth to community, the congregation will now sadly be saying goodbye. Rev. Barth was pronounced dead three days ago, cause of death unknown, and has been buried in Cedarburg Cemetery during a private funeral with no relatives in the area, he will now rest alone and in peace. Congregation is devastated by the loss of this beloved pastor...

Most of this was useless. My shed was on Murdock Road, meaning I lived next to the brothel-turned-farmhouse where two murders took place decades ago. It didn't help my situation any, but it was nice to learn I chose a home with some history. It seemed fitting in a way, considering my circumstances.

The only thing that stood out to me as useful was the article about Revered Christian Barth—no known cause of death, no family, private burial. It could be nothing, but it seemed out of place for a pastor who was so beloved by his congregation to just sort of die and disappear like that. His church, St. James used to be the Catholic Parish, and was the same church I heard the screams from a few days before.

It struck me as odd that the strange circumstances surrounding this deceased man were home to the only building that held some significance to me in this town. Correlation did not mean causation, of course, but it was the only thing I found that held a chance of leading to some answers.

I glanced out the window and on the corner by the bus stop stood a young kid, probably about seventeen. He wore a trench coat and his hands were stuffed deep inside the pockets; he was probably peddling drugs. Not exactly what I expected from this white suburbia, but I suppose every town has their secrets. I watched him fidget with whatever it was he clung so desperately to in his pockets and thought about sucking on his neck. It wasn't sexy like in a mortal way. No, in unlife, the appetite for blood replaces any sexual appetite.

I erased the search history, closed out of the browser, and pulled out my phone. I sent a text to Sage asking her to meet up later, and then I crawled back out the broken window and put on my sweatshirt, creeping around the building toward my next meal.

He made himself an easy target. Some punk ass kid who thought he was tough shit. He'd be on the bottom of the totem pole tonight. I pulled my hood down and stuffed my hands in my pockets, much like he did, and adopted a nervous fidget.

"Uh, hey man...you uh, you got anything I can get from you?" I said.

"What kinda shit you lookin' for?"

"Uh, I mean..." I cleared my throat, "what kinda shit you got?"

He looked past me toward the road. "Come over here for a sec and I'll show you. I ain't want no cars to see nothin'."

Impeccable grammar, really. But it's okay; he led himself right into a trap. My trap. And that's all that mattered.

Around the corner of the library, he opened his trench coat and reached into an inside pocket. I leaned forward, pretending to get a peek, and lunged at him. Grabbed his stubbled face and plunged my fangs into his smooth, pale neck. He started to yell, but before he made more than a burp of sound, I shoved my fingers in his mouth and gagged him. His tongue sloshed around and his eyes got wide with panic. He struggled against me and as I drank, a great thrill blossomed within me.

Soon enough, he was complacent. He just stood there, letting me suck on his neck. His blood had a musty taste to it, like a grandparent's attic, but blood was blood and I was thirsty.

After my thirst was satiated, I let him go and his body fell to the ground. He was awake but weak, and looked up at me like I was some white Colombian smack. On an impulse, I reached inside his coat pocket and nicked the little baggies of drugs. His eyes followed me as I examined them. And then I dumped the contents out and stomped them into the ground.

I looked at him and shrugged. "Oops."

Halfway back to my shed, I got a reply from Sage.

I'll meet you at your place. Better not be pointless.

Yeah, she didn't hate me.

Chapter Seven

I STOOD OUTSIDE AND WAITED FOR HER arrival. Two owls called back and forth to each other lackadaisically. After a few minutes of listening in on their conversation and watching the moon weave in and out of the passing clouds, I spotted Sage walking down the road.

"This better not be a waste of my time," she said as she crossed the street.

"I know about the ring."

She stopped in the middle of the road and looked at me with her slit-like pupils now bulging and wide. "How do you know about that?"

"Annabelle."

"How do you know her?" She sounded nervous.

"Does it matter? I got information out of her. Doesn't that make me worthy? She attacked me and I still got her to tell me about the ring."

I was a bad liar. Sage pushed past me and invited herself inside. She scoffed. My lie didn't get past her.

"Good for you Maaria, you know about the ring. Everyone knows about the ring. Tell me something I don't know."

"Something you don't know? Okay. That old church, St. James? A pastor died there in 1921. He was only there for two years, no known cause of death, no family, a private funeral. But he was—and I quote—a beloved pastor."

"So? A pastor died and no one attended his funeral. Who cares?"

"You're telling me a beloved pastor of a church dies and his own congregation not hearing about it until he's already buried is totally normal? Not suspicious at all? I mean, it might not have anything to do with the ring, but it's the only thing that stands out to me. And if you really want to keep this ring away from the Primus, it'd probably be a good idea to be more thorough than you think you need to be."

The corners of her eyes tightened as she glared at me in silence. Key words there—in silence. No smart-ass comments. That's how I knew I said the right thing. It was so silent I could hear the soft pitter-patter of a rat's paws outside, walking a schizophrenic little path. It must have lost its little rat family or been searching for something it had lost.

"Okay. Let's go."

My attention snapped back to Sage. "Go where?"

"The church," she said.

I was stunned. Speechless.

She reached in her pocket and threw a silver object toward me. I instinctively reached out and caught it. Opening my hand, there was a silver stake resting in my palm. It was plain, unadorned, just a few lines etched along the handle.

"It's obviously not one hundred percent," Sage said.

"Percent what?" I looked up, still in a mild state of shock.

"Silver."

My mind took me floating back to a memory. Back with Mornor when he cleared up all the vampiric myths. Our final death only came with fire or sun. The myth of a stake to the heart was only a half-truth. And the myth about silver being poison to us held even less truth.

'It isn't,' Mornor had said. 'We are just allergic to it. Only an object of pure silver, one hundred percent, will affect us. Just irritate us a little, burn some, cause a little pain. But it's not going to poison us. And it surely doesn't kill us.'

A whistle brought me back to reality.

"Well," Sage said and waved a hand at me. "Let's go."

We walked side by side, but stared straight ahead.

"You shouldn't trust her," Sage said.

"I don't. But she hasn't exactly proven to be a real threat, either."

She responded only with silence.

"I know the Primus is the leader of the Nobilis Sanguis," I said, trying to change to subject. "And I know he wants the ring, but...I don't know, I guess I don't understand why."

Sage shot a glance at me from the corner of her eye. "The Primus is the leader of the Nobilis Sanguis, yes. They're all Valde, and among the race, only a select few are inducted into the faction. The Royal Blood, they're called. They're the ones that are Awakened with inherent abilities...like you," she added begrudgingly. "The Primus is mad, absolutely batshit, old, drunk on power. And he recalled some time when the ring was brought here by some vampire. And he wants it. Why? I don't think we can ever really know for sure. But I can only assume it's for power. It's all political corruption, the Nobilis Sanguis. Just a bunch of aristocratic pricks.

"If we want to stop him, we need as much help as we can find. He's got a whole faction behind him—or what's left of it—and there aren't many of us left. So we're forced to pick up the scraps we can find. Nobody wants to show up and help, though."

"Yet you won't work with Annabelle."

A smile crossed her face. The kind of smile that meant she was going to make you feel real bad about yourself.

"She doesn't even respect you enough to tell you her Awakened name?"

I ignored the question and asked, "Does every vampire have an Awakened name?"

"Way to dodge the question," she said. "But no. Some choose one themselves, some are given to them by their Sire, some simply keep their mortal name. Some don't remember their name so they just pick a new one."

"So you and I?"

"Mornor gives each of his Childs a second name, always pertaining to night or darkness. Because we belong to it now, the night. That's what Nyx means—night."

"Born at night," I said. "Maaria, Born at Night."

And there I was again, in that empty room, minutes after I Awoke. The first glance out the window into the night, where the crescent moon lit the whole sky. Part terror, part tranquility, and part exhilaration. A piece of me yearned to go back there just then. Everything was easier when I was with Mornor. It seemed likely that he was the only one who actually cared about me.

"That's not the only thing we have in common," Sage said. "I told you I had an opium addiction. I know you were addicted to something too. He only Awakens mortals with a drug dependency, gives us a second chance."

"I was a heroin addict," I responded. "Or so he told me. I don't remember it. I don't remember anything from my life."

An intimate silence passed between us.

"Why are you doing this?" I said. "What made you suddenly change your mind about me?"

I never got an answer.

Her arm flew to her side. For some reason I thought she was going to grab her stake and plunge it into me.

"Whoa, hey now," I protested.

She gave me a venomous look and pushed a finger to her lips. "Shut up," she hissed.

When she brought her hand out from her coat, it wasn't a stake. It was a machete. Large and rusty, but sharp as hell. She focused down the road where the church stood. A beam of light poured out from inside.

"You need a machete?" I hissed. "It could be a mortal."

She scoffed. "The day I see a mortal in a church outside the hours of ten to eleven on a Sunday morning is the day the undead will rule the world."

I couldn't argue with that.

"Can I trust you with something?" she said.

I nodded.

"Take this," she said and pulled the ring off her finger. "Shadow yourself. Just twist it once and it will obey whatever you intend for it to do. I'm going in there. You stay here."

"You're sure?" I asked.

But only the wind heard me. She was already walking toward the church. And then she disappeared, blending in with the night-drenched earth.

I put the ring on my finger with as much reverence as I could muster and twisted it, marveling at the silver light of the moon glinting off the black gem. And then it was gone. A shadow was cast over me, just as I had intended. A blue-black hue darkened my pale hands.

I crept closer to the church and peered through one of the windows. Inside, I saw two men dressed in matching suit and tie—one with a flashlight—searching the church. Uprooting pews, flipping through hymnal pages, tossing communion ware all over. Behind them, I saw a flash of moonbeam against a levitating blade. It swayed through the air and then disappeared behind the man with the flashlight. A second later, it was jutting out through his chest.

He and the flashlight dropped to the floor. Dead. The machete wrenched itself from the lifeless body.

I crouched beneath the window and twisted the ring again and with it, the light of the flashlight went out. Peering through the bottom corner of the window, the blade pointed toward me with appreciation.

This all happened in the blink of an eye and the other man whipped himself around with a gun drawn, pointing it in the direction of where the light had gone out. His dead comrade. Sage was quicker than him, though, and was already creeping toward him, out of sight.

He couldn't have been a vampire. He would've seen the blade floating toward him, even with the absence of light. He would have heard the footsteps that resounded with decibels well below the human threshold of sound.

With a leap, the machete whirled through the air and the man turned, pointing his gun. But he was too late. The blade swung down right through his neck. His thick head, with beady, frightened eyes, fell to the floor, bouncing a few times before settling into its resting place.

Within seconds, Sage was outside, running around the building with wide eyes and muttering curses under her breath.

"Let's go," she breathed.

And we ran.

"What were those?" I said.

Her eyes shot that familiar fiery look at me. "What were those? That's what you're asking me right now. What were those."

"Yeah. It is." I said.

"Don't you think we have some bigger things to worry about than 'what were those?' There are two dead and mutilated bodies in that church right now. That's not going to go unnoticed. Fucking Christ, Maaria."

I didn't speak again until we were back in the safety of my shed. Or at least I had hoped it was safe. You could never really know, I guess.

Sage sat at the desk chair again, head in her hands.

"Ghouls," she said. "Those were ghouls. Blood slaves. Whatever you want to call them. Feed a little vampire blood to a mortal, get them addicted to it, and they're yours. They'll do anything you ask of them."

"Who do you think they work for, the Primus?"

"I can only imagine, yes." She looked up at me. "Which means they've been one step ahead of us.

Which means we need a new lead. They'll know someone has the same idea as them. They'll know someone was looking for the ring. If they find out who we are, they'll kill us. They'll fucking kill us, Maaria."

"We don't know that," I said. "In our favor, maybe they won't use the church anymore—the mortals— after a double homicide. So we could sneak in there anytime."

"Jesus Christ, Maaria."

I offered a poor attempt at an apologetic smile, but she simply got up and left.

"Text me in a day or two," she said as she walked out the door and closed it behind her.

She was right. Not only were there two dead bodies in the church—which would mean an investigation— but now the Primus would know other vampires had been there. It would make things a lot more difficult for us.

But I knew then, as well as I know now, she had to kill them. If they had found something there and went back to the Primus with it, we would be even worse off than we were. We'd have to lay low and find something else that would give us an advantage. And it seemed hopeless.

But I realized—maybe this was my purpose. Finding the ring, saving us from the tyranny of the Nobilis Sanguis.

THE NEXT NIGHT, I CREPT THROUGH THE trees and out to the church. It was surrounded by police tape—two police cars still there, lights off and flashlights on. Whether they were keeping watch or searching for missed evidence, I didn't know. Nor did I care. I went back to my shed. We would have to wait. Wait until it all blew over and we were able to search for more. If anything, it gave us some time to think. And if we couldn't get into the church at all, I knew the Primus wouldn't be able to either. Like both Sage and Annabelle had said—he's delusional. But he wasn't stupid. He knew he couldn't let mortals know about our already fragile existence. It wasn't just a rule—it was self-preservation.

I waited four days before texting Sage. She was still keeping her guard up about the whole thing, but if the Nobilis Sanguis had any idea who was there that night, we would have been dead already; or at least kidnapped, attacked—something. They apparently weren't the type to give you the silent treatment, they'd attack and they'd do it with a dramatic presence.

'Inflated egos,' Sage had told me one night and she ballooned her hands around her head. This was going to be a war now, we were sure of it. And finally, Sage decided she would train me for battle.

This went on for almost two weeks—training me in new abilities, looking for information in useless places, feeding. That was our lives. The only three things it consisted of.

"Aura reading," Sage said one night. "You know what it is, I hope."

I nodded.

"Well, now you'll learn how to do it."

For nights I trained, straining the powers of my mind, attempting to connect to this conscious and psychic substance that flowed through me.

Sage had told me—as well as Mornor—that it was our blood. Wherever our origins lie, it began with the blood. It was transferred through the blood, it lived in the blood, it became the blood. Our bodies died, but were animated by this something in the blood. This something was more than just a chemical reaction, more than the mortals' choice word, supernatural, could explain. Mornor had said that it was 'alive, something with a force of will and a mind of its own.'
Over the millennia, our race had come to realize this, to understand it. And then, to utilize it, to develop their own powers and abilities; harnessed through the

power, force, and will that inherently lies in our blood, dormant aside from the animation it graces us with.

So for nights I focused on harnessing this power, until one night, I could see the pale glow of pink-white light around Sage's body.

"There it is," I said, pointing at it.

That was the first time I had ever seen a genuine smile cross her face. Not a malicious smile, not a sarcastic smile, a smile with warmth. A smile that was almost human. And I realized that when Annabelle had told me Sage still felt the bonds of family, even in unlife, she mustn't have been lying.

We weren't just blood relation anymore, we were family—by blood or not. She truly saw me as her sister now. Whether she knew it or not.

After I'd mastered aura reading—an ability only used by the Myagoros—I went to practice it on a mortal. All vampires had the same pink-white aura, the radiating energy of that something in our blood. I could only assume the paleness of it was a result of our existence without life. Mortals had a much more varied and vibrant aura. The aura of the mortal I found in the park glowed a deep forest green—electric and neon. I felt almost ashamed as I left him there, lying next to the swings, because after I'd taken so much, his aura was a sickly pastel mint.

As I walked back, I heard a soft purr from the trees. "Hello, Maaria."

I whipped around and spotted the glowing yellow eyes. I kept walking.

"That was you wasn't it? The other night in the church. You killed those precious little blood slaves."

I stopped and turned back. Her eyes studied me.

"Oh, so it was Sage. But you were there," she said with a poke of her temple. There was blood coated on the underside of her fingernail.

"Who'd you kill tonight?"

"Hah, you're funny. I don't kill everyone, Maaria; there are only so many people in this town. I can't have anyone thinking there's some sick fuck of a serial killer around. That would ruin all the fun."

"Riiight."

She stared back at me with an expression of innocence, waiting for something more.

"If we find anything, yes, I will let you know," I said.

Something between a grimace and a beaming smile spread across her face. "Don't seem so eager to help," she said. "You and Sage have become buddies now haven't you?" She scraped the blood from under her fingernail with her teeth.

I rolled my eyes. "I said I'd help you. What does it matter?"

She shrugged. "It doesn't. How about you give me your phone number." Not a request—a demand. "I mean, unless you want me following you around, so I can keep in touch with you?"

I shook my head. "You are unbelievable."

"Sure. So, your number."

I hesitated, but complied and rattled it off.

"You should get back to your little research project before the Primus does," she said. "I heard he has a Regency appointed to do all his dirty work."

"What are you doing to keep this ring out of his hands?" I asked.

"I do my part." And with a wink and a smirk, she twisted her ring and her black fog cloaked her.

I went home to train until sunrise, but it was futile. Annabelle's words kept tugging at my sleeve, fighting for my attention. A Regency. Sage hadn't said anything about a Regency. Did she know?

Immediately following my mastery of aura reading, Sage went on to teach me another. The ability she used so often—hiding oneself in plain sight, blending in with your surroundings, adopting the likeness of a chameleon. This ability took longer to learn. I'd often change my appearance, but look like grass attempting to blend into a wooden wall or vice versa. After a few days I got better at it, but I would sometimes choose the wrong shade.

After accomplishing the ability we moved right on to the next. No breaks. This was making a small object invisible. A handy ability if we ever did end up finding this ring. Sage and I sat in my shed for hours one night. Attempt after attempt to make various pebbles dis-appear. And as I trained, Sage talked.

"I've told you what the Shrine believes, but not what they do." Sage let out a sigh.

I believe every Awakened carries some mortal habit over into unlife and this was hers. Sighing. Breath.

"Lilitu is our Mother. The Mother of vampires, werewolves, shapeshifters, anything undead or evil, anything supernatural. Our very existence is attributed to this demon. The Shrine offers sacrifices to her, performs rituals in her name—anything to appease her, thank her, praise her for allowing us to exist. They offer the same things to pagan gods too; they think they're under the rule of Lilitu and act as our active guardians. The Shrine believes it's our duty to—"

"Do you really believe that?" I interrupted. "It seems like an excuse to believe in something, same as mortals. If you ask me, there are no gods, no one is allowing us to exist. We just are."

The small stone in my palm vanished.

"A surprising amount of vampires believe it. I don't. But the Shrine holds a power. Their magic works, the ancients understood something about our blood that we've lost. Anyway, when I was with them in Chicago they had appointed me as an Initiator. I really shouldn't have been, considering I don't believe an ounce of what they say, but—"

"Initiator?" I asked. I folded my fingers into my palm, feeling the invisible stone, solid as ever.

"There's an order to the Shrine. Any vampire can join and offer up their sacrifices, but if you want to learn any of their rituals, there's an initiation process. It's a way to weed out all the followers who don't believe in Lilitu and who are just after the only useful part about the creed—the rituals. Unbelievers don't learn them. Unless you lie."

Her familiar smirk quivered on the side of her lips and threatened to break out into a prideful grin. But before her lips could betray her, she continued.

"You collect the blood of all your sacrifices to Lilitu and bathe in it. They call it bathing in your Red Sea. An appointed Leader or Initiator speaks certain rites over you while you bathe. It's a binding contract between the Awakened and the Mother. It's bullshit is all it is, but there's a lot of vampires who are stupid enough to believe there's actually power in those words. Granted, I'm sure there would be if Lilitu actually existed and was our Mother. But I took the oath and haven't gotten cursed for my lack of respect, so I think it's safe to say she's not real. Whatever." She looked me in the eyes and said, "You gather some blood, I initiate you, and you get to learn a few more trick. What do you say?"

Chapter Eight

THUNDER BOOMED THROUGHOUT THE sky, shaking the frame of the shed and rattling the remains of the old brothel-turned-farmhouse. Lightning flashed in a hectic fashion. Dancing chaotically and forming asymmetrical patterns across the sky. Sage arrived a half hour later as rained poured down in solid sheets. In her hands she carried glass jars and plastic jugs, all filled with the blood we'd collected from animals we killed. These were our sacrifices to Lilitu. And that night, I would be initiated into her Shrine.

There was still a small, rusty bathtub inside the house's remains that I would bathe in. I wondered if it was the same tub the poor Madame had been drowned in all those years ago. As Sage walked over, her eyes were electrified by each flash of lightning, an intensity passing through them. Without a word, she walked past me and through the blackened doorframe of the house. We poured the blood into the bath and I stepped down. My porcelain skin would have matched the color of the tub had it not been painted with so much decay.

I stepped into it and lowered my naked body into the pool of blood. It was thick, stale, and cold. I let my arms by my side and watched the blood seep over my hands. I couldn't help but think about my mortal death, lying in a dirty tub. There was a certain symbolism to be found in this moment. Death and rebirth, in every sense of the words. I tilted my head back over the edge of the tub and the cold, hard rain pelted my face. Sage stood over me and placed her right hand on my bare chest where my heart should have been beating, but instead, lay dormant and shriveled.

She spoke forebodingly—all drama—and in a foreign tongue.

"Ae ma a, d'ya heb, b'k ha yae." She reached her left hand towards the sky. "Ae noa, oa aob'elo, b'k ha yae." She placed it on my shoulder. "B'eh obad moa, ae noa, kia yin." She wiped blood across my chest. "B'eh obad moa, ae noa, dam da'k yoa." She smeared blood on my face. "Ae ma a, d'al yalu odea, obad moa, aasu or, k'ay." She made an inverted cross, starting at my throat and ending down just below my breasts. "L'hal akh ra yoa, aemu ot." She pushed down on my chest. "Ae noa, obad moa." She smeared blood on my stomach. "Ae noa, od'i yil, b'eh ae ma a." She looked up toward the sky.

Her hands rested on my shoulders and she pushed me down into the blood until my face was submerged into my Red Sea.

"Oshak ra a," she said. "Drink."

I gulped down the bitter blood until the pressure of her hands was gone from my shoulders. I rose up. I felt no different. I felt as if the rain should have stopped, the sky cleared up, like some sort of theatrical finale to a melodramatic ritual. But nothing happened. I felt not even the slightest tingle.

"That's it?" I said.

"A bit underwhelming, yes. The Shrine tends to be a little theatrical. They really glorify that occult aesthetic."

I stepped out of the tub and allowed the rain to wash the rest of the blood off my body before I pulled on my drenched clothes that lay in a heap at my feet.

"You are now baptized in the blood," Sage smirked.

We sat in my shed the rest of the night talking about the various rituals the Shrine had formulated since its manifestation. As I listened to Sage speak, I began to appreciate her attitude of irreverence. It seemed to be the overriding theme to this damned existence—the cardinal rule. Treat everything with an ample dose of irreverence. Looking back, Mornor had carried the same predisposition.

The night before he departed he told me:

'One final piece of advice, my sweet Maaria. I believe the mortals say, a spoonful of sugar helps the medicine go down? Forget that. The medicine is poison, it always is. Just lies. Anything vampires do to make this existence seem more bearable is the very thing that will lead to their inevitable demise.

'A spoonful of venom will keep you immune to those snakes, Maaria. Remember that. Always remain skeptical. Take things with a spoonful of cynicism, not sugar. Never give in to the piety, no matter how tempting.'

The next night, Sage and I no longer dwelled on this topic, but focused on the rituals. She told me about the five common rituals of the creed; how there could have been more but they were kept secret, the knowledge of them only made available to those of a much higher status than herself. Or perhaps they were just lost to the passing of time, swept away by the hands of the clock, buried beneath the sands of the great hourglass.

For all the Shrine's emphasis on aesthetic, the names of the rituals weren't the least bit creative. They were called Ring of Darkness, Black Plague, Living Shadow, Poison Stone, and Rune Caster. Of these, Sage knew only three.

"You'll only be able to learn one ritual right now," Sage said. "One of them is easy enough once you've got all the necessary ingredients, but catching a bat is easier said than done."

"What about the other?" I asked.

"You'll need the ashes of what used to be one of us. Not easy to come by. And I would rather not give the final death to someone who doesn't deserve it. Like I said, there aren't many of us left."

"So what rituals are those for? The bat and the ashes?"

"The bat is for Living Shadow. You perform the ritual right, you become just what it's called—a living shadow. For a whole twenty-four hours you'll be unharmed by sunlight. It's useful, but there are better things to do with your time, I think. The ashes are for Ring of Darkness," she wiggled her fingers. "Do a ritual that compresses them into a jewel, pop it on a ring, and you can control—you guessed it—shadows and darkness."

I hesitated. "Whose ashes did you use?"

She shrugged. "I'm not sure. I didn't know him. About ten years after I was Awakened I was with a small coven of Shrine members. They were quarreling with some nearby group of vampires and this guy waltzed over one night and they killed him. They all had rings already so they gave me the ashes to make my own."

I didn't know if I believed it, but it didn't really matter either way. It made no difference now.

"You'll be learning Black Plague," she said.

The ritual was simple. A black beetle crushed in sight of your unfortunate target would blacken and stiffen their skin, like a rigor mortis effect. All you needed for the ritual to take effect—other than the beetle—was the recite a little spell. We walked outside and Sage found us a beetle within a few minutes.

"This will hurt a bit," she said. "It's more startling than painful, really. The effects will only last about ten minutes. It's simple, but to the unsuspecting, it can be pretty useful."

I nodded and readied my stance. As if widening my legs and bending at the knees would somehow make this less of a shock. This was my mortal tendency. The subconscious little things all mortals did, which do nothing physically, but provide them with some sort of mental relief.

I pursed my lips in a thin smile.

"Pay attention to the spell. I'm not going to write it down, so memorize it."

I nodded again. I felt nervous, but it was a peculiar feeling because there was no sick tinge in my stomach, just a little itch in my brain that echoed the feeling. So strange, being undead can be.

"Ready?" said Sage.

"Ready."

"Okay. Nigrum scarabaeus. Nigra cutis. Nigrum scarabaeus. Nigrum pestis. Deos inficiunt aspiciet inimica mea. In nomine Lilitu. In nomine Lilitu."

Her fingers crushed the beetle and the dust of the carcass gently spilled onto the ground. With the last word and the last of the dust, the blackness crept up my arm.

It started in my fingertips and skidded up my arms like sprouting roots. I held my arm out and stared at it. Nearly all blackened, I could no longer move or feel it; a strange constriction like my limb had contracted so greatly that it was incapable of moving on even a molecular level. My arm seemed to be the most solid object in existence.

"Simple," said Sage, "but effective."

I scoffed. "You could say that."

She smiled.

"What does it mean?" I asked.

"The spell? Black beetle. Black skin. Black beetle. Black plague. Gods, infect my enemy. In the name of Lilitu. In the name of Lilitu."

She walked inside and I followed. There was a dull pain in my arm, but it was the sheer strangeness of it that caught me off guard. Talk of the ring distracted me while we waited for the effects to wear off.

There are things I wanted to ask Sage yet, things I knew she had the answers to. Like, who was in the church the night I met her? Whose remains did the pile of ash I found belong to? What was this Regency the Primus had appointed? But this wasn't the time to ask such things. I didn't want to press her while she mentored me. I feared if she were angry, she would run off again. And I needed her. So I told myself the questions could wait.

Once feeling returned to my arm and it was porcelain again, we ventured back outside. I found myself a beetle and got ready to recite the spell and perform the ritual on Sage.

She was right when she said the spell was easy—it didn't take more than the correct pronunciation. I made sure to mutter it as quietly as possibly, less than a whisper, per Sage's instructions. The spell had to stay inside the Shrine.

"Why?" I asked her. "I thought you find their beliefs silly. What does it matter if non-Shrine members know the spell?"

"It's not so much the rule, but the fact that I don't want anyone else to know it."

And with nothing more to learn that night, we parted ways and decided to meet again in a few nights to check on the church. It had been too long. Sure, we needed to stay safe and out of attention, but it was more important to stay one step ahead of the Primus. Or at least keep pace with him.

Chapter Nine

I'M ON MY WAY OVER.

It was two nights later. I hoped Sage's text meant we would be heading to the church. Since we'd last been there, a new Sage was revealed to me. She trusted me; saw me as a worthy vampire, a worthy Child of Mornor. And I was absolutely certain she finally came to see me as family. I don't know what spurred it; I never tried to ask again. I was curious, but would knowing the reason really make any difference? Probably not.

I came to see her as a sister as well. But it was more than just seeing her as a sister—she felt like one. Every-thing about our relationship changed so quickly. It had grown from a sapling to a fully-grown oak, towering over all other trees. We shared an undeniable bond, a something in our blood.

We were sisters.

The door opened. The magic flame flickered in Sage's eyes as she walked in.

"Wanna go feed on campus tonight?"

I smiled. "Let's go."

Conversation was nonexistent as we trekked toward the school. But you better believe that I noticed how Sage ran beside me now, not in front of me. It was just another testimony to her affinity toward me. Our feet stepped in perfect rhythm as we walked along the road that circled the campus grounds. The small itch of thirst in me was quickly becoming an incessant drone and it was hard to focus. Sage growled and nudged me, nodding ahead toward the parking structure. Two boys were stumbling out. One big and bearded and the other tall and lanky, both loud with robust laughter and a jaunty gait. Again, thank god for alcohol.

One was shouting, "...You know? And I—I—I—I—I...I don't even eat cakes!"

The other roared with laughter at this and Sage and I fell behind them, sulking in the shadows like your stereotypical emo vampire kid. And it was that simple.

They struggled at first, like most mortals do, but after a few moments—like all mortals—they lost enough blood to give up fighting. Their struggle was weaker than most. Blame it on the alcohol. When we finished, we ripped out our fangs, turned, and ran back the way we came.

I looked back at them. The big one swayed, threatening to fall over and the tall one had dropped to the sidewalk with his chin drooping over his chest.

I turned forward and Sage wiped the blood from her chin. I did the same. Call it common courtesy. From behind us I heard one of the boys slurring.

"W—whoa there, whad you put in thoss drinks there, buddy!" A drunken hiccup was followed by chuckle that faded into drunken defeat.

As we left, I veered off in the direction of the church and Sage didn't protest. The thrill of blood had left us feeling invincible. And this feeling will so often leave you being careless. We trotted off the grounds and passed right through the shining headlights of an SUV in the parking lot.

I glanced back nervously. "You think they saw us?"

Sage scoffed. "What does it matter? What are they going to do, kill us?"

"Yeah...no, you're right." Though I wasn't completely convinced.

Once I reached the road, I steered off into the ditch, keeping hidden by the overgrown brush. Sage did it purely out of habit, but I was still worried about the vehicle. Most likely, it did belong to a mortal;

someone returning to campus or preparing to leave. It wasn't that late in the night yet.

The road brightened. Headlights. The streetlights above us burst and sparks showered down. Sage had twisted her ring. We crouched low and the light intensified. Looking ahead, I could see the church already. No lights, no cars, no police tape. I breathed a mental sigh of relief.

The soft roar of tires on pavement rushed past us. A red sedan. I breathed a second mental sigh of relief while Sage let out an audible one. I gave her an accusing look.

"Shut up," she mumbled.

We continued toward the church when a second glow of headlights flashed behind us. With nowhere to hide this time, Sage twisted the ring and threw a shadow over us.

A black Escalade sped down the road. Passed us.

Slammed on the brakes and pulled over.

"Shit."

The passenger door swung open and a cold laugh infected the air.

"You think you can hide from us that easy?" Two men in suits walked out of the vehicle, both of them wielding guns. The one who spoke was tall and broad, the other thin and wiry.

Sage stepped forward with her hand ready to draw her machete from under her coat. "You think those little guns of yours threaten us? I can easily get you to talk, you know. Give me information about your precious Primus. Don't think you can try and test me you pathetic…little ghouls."

The broad one grimaced. "Look at your eyes. You're no Valde. I am not afraid of you."

"I don't need to be a Valde," she chuckled and drew her machete. "You know what I did to your little pals. All I need is this." She swung the blade at her side and the ghouls just stared at us, expressionless. The wiry one began to fidget.

He cleared his throat. "The uh…the Primus. He knows—"

A bullet shot through his head. Dropped to the ground. Dead.

"You're going to kill him for that?" yelled Sage.

He shrugged and lowered the gun. "It's not our job to talk," he said.

"Then what are you here for?"

He smirked. "Tread carefully."

"Oh. We will." Light glinted off her blade as she swung it and charged toward him. He brought his gun up again. But instead of pointing it at Sage, he jammed the barrel into his mouth and pulled the trigger.

Blood and brain matter splattered the asphalt. Sage jumped back as the body crumpled on the road. She glanced back at me with wide eyes, but jerked back and up to the body, prying the gun from his hand and bringing it over to me.

"Here, take it. I except you'll need it."

I wrapped my hand around it and inspected it. I'd never used a gun before. At least not that I could remember.

"Why did he do it?" I asked.

"I don't know," she shrugged and fell into a troubled silence.

I was just as confused.

"What about the church?"

But she was already walking away.

"Hey!" I yelled at her. "What about—"

"What about it?" She stopped and turned back. "There are two more dead bodies, Maaria. The church can wait another night."

She was right of course, like usual, but it hadn't made it any easier to accept the fact that we were losing ground every night we didn't spend searching for information. And we had to assume the Primus was looking for information every night, or had someone doing it for him. Like the ghouls. The blood slaves. The Regency.

Why did he kill himself? God, it bothered me so much. Had he been ordered to do it? Perhaps the Primus was trying to send a message—that the ghouls would do anything he asked of them. I didn't know. How could I know? But I didn't need to understand him; I just needed to find the ring.

And I didn't even know why.

I chose to be a part of a war for reasons I didn't have. I very well could have chosen to just ignore all of it; to not get involved in any way. But by this point it was too late. I had made my choice. It was a choice part of me regrets ever making, but another part of me knows I never really had a real choice in the matter. It was made for me.

After this, I knew the Primus—or someone within the Nobilis Sanguis—knew who I was. Knew where to find us. Anxiety made sleep seem impossible, but in a few hours the sun would rise above the horizon and it would drag me down in a deep slumber, like a dead man in the grave.

And so I sat in my shed, alone as ever, and practiced these new abilities of mine, familiarized myself with this gun. It was far too late to back out of this. And I was determined to prepare myself for whatever may come.

UNDER THE STEEL BLUE LIGHT OF THE MOON, I went out and fed on the creatures that dwelled in the woods. Human blood was so much more gratifying, and the hunt provided an inexorable thrill, but I found the trees and the life within them comforting.

I thought it harsh to make me choose between this comfort I so enjoyed and the thrill that my nature desired. And the already present struggle between human and monster—which I stupidly thought I'd rid myself of—made it altogether cruel to make me choose between satisfaction and simple necessity. I loved the natural order of the woods, but craved the sadism in feeding from my own. Not really my own, but mortals (in a sense) are just a hair's breadth away from cannibalism.

We're similar aliens—vampires and humans. Surprisingly alike, yet completely different animals. Some-times I forgot I was no longer one of them. Sure, we might look a little different, but we still share the same human form, just a little modified. But if you took away all that, all the obvious vampiric qualities— change in appearance, pale skin, fangs, nocturnal, blood drinking, et cetera—then no one could tell us apart. The good and evil parts of us grip us both. The person we want to be, fighting against the part of us we don't want to admit is there. Take away appearance and the behaviors us undead have no control over, and we're the same. It's not man versus monster. We both feel. And feeling looks identical in everyone. We have emotions. We struggle with them. Strip away the outside, the superficial, and we're both just the product of good and evil, black and white. We're all grey on the inside. We're all motivated by the same desires.

But our greatest motivator is where we differ. Mortals are motivated by death; they have this tiny timeframe and they have to do everything they want before the reaper comes to collect their toll. Vampires, we're motivated by boredom. We've got an eternity to sit on our ass. It's no wonder so many vampires go mad.

And it's funny because I see so many mortals doing everything they can to escape their reality. But if they knew what it meant to actually escape it, if they knew what it meant to be undead, they'd beg for their life back. But would they? Did I want to be mortal? Not really. It seemed pretty shitty. But I'm not really one to speak, am I? I don't remember it; don't know what being human is really like. But just like the search for the ring, it was too late to go back now. A vampire now and forevermore.

Back in my shed I stretched my control of my abilities. I had progressed from making small pebbles invisible to rocks the size of my hand. With mastery of the ability, you could presumably make an object the size of an infant disappear. I still had a long way to go, but I was advancing quickly.

It was a quiet night. Only one car had wheeled down my little stretch of road. I thought I'd step outside and give Sage a call, wondering if she would want to go to the church, since the opportunity unfortunately escaped us the previous night. I heard the hum of a car driving down the street and waited for it to pass. But it didn't. It only stopped.

A familiar tremor of fear seeped from bones and sent my skin crawling. I pulled the door open a crack and peered through the sliver of space. A black Escalade sat on the side of the street closest me, but the driver's side was facing me like it had been driving down the wrong side of the road.

The door opened and a bouquet of long brown curls poured out. They hung over a face with impossibly smooth skin and high cheekbones, and ever so delicately brushed against his shoulders. He wore black jeans and a flannel. Not a ghoul. He would have been wearing a suit if he was—or more importantly—if he was a ghoul that worked for the Primus. He looked mortal aside from the gorgeously chiseled face. Not even Photoshop could have worked that magic. I'd never seen anything quite like him.

Even though I was almost positive he wasn't a ghoul, I closed my eyes and let the paranormal essence well up inside me. When I opened them, I peered through the crack and saw the pale glow of a vampire's aura around him. I backed away. He was a Lussuro then—the appearance of a mortal, just with a beauty that was beyond even the most exquisite humans.

It confused me. He drove an Escalade like he was working for the Primus, but I thought the Nobilis Sanguis was solely vampires of the Royal Blood. And those were only members of the Valde race, not the Lussuro or anyone else.

A knock at the door sent a small panic rising up in me. A mental struggle gripped me—do I open the door or not. Curiosity got the best of me.

I swung the door open and threw an unconvincing reaction of mild surprise at him.

"Umm…uh, hey," I stuttered.

The corner of his lip curled up in a charming smile and he said, "Maaria, I presume?"

"Yeah. Yup. That's…that's me."

He offered the same smile. "I'm Gabriel. And my boss would like to meet you."

My brows furrowed in suspicion, but this was washed away by trust. He pulled an envelope from his pocket, unfolded the letter and he read:

"This is an official summons from the order of Serafino, to one Maaria Naeva. On this night of October 18, you are invited to the West Gate Bank, located in Milwaukee, Wisconsin, to discuss the notions of a future business opportunity. Should you deny the invitation, you will be subject to any manner of action normally reserved for our enemies. However, should you graciously accept this invitation, you will be treated as an ally and be graced with many rewards. Signed, Serafino—Head of the Regency."

He looked up and his eyes drilled into mine again as he waited for my response. But I was lost in my thoughts for a moment.

A small voice in the back of my head kept saying: Don't go. Don't trust him. But it was muffled and broken, like a phone call with poor reception. The voice didn't convince me and the trust I felt for Gabriel won, completely overwhelming all reason. But logic said something different. Logic told me Go, because they didn't really give me a choice.

"Okay," I said.

He beamed back at me and in the parting of his lips, he revealed a set of beautiful, snow-white fangs.

"Come with me, then."

Chapter Ten

E OPENED THE CAR DOOR FOR ME AND I sat in the seat behind him. "Pepper," by the Butthole Surfers droned out from the stereo. He drove silently, not speaking a word since the key turned in the ignition. My phone vibrated in my pocket. I took it out carefully and held it between my knees to read the message. I was from Annabelle.

I'm waiting.

She wanted information, some kind of update on the ring. I was trying to put off telling her anything, but I knew I'd have to sooner or later. I'd tell her as little as I could and hope—just hope—that she would trust me and not go prying inside my head for something more.

I texted her back:

Meet me tomorrow. The gazebo on the edge of campus.

I don't know why I chose to meet her there. There was really no reason for it. I saw it standing out there and thought it sort of pretty, sort of secluded. Plus, I didn't want her to know where I lived. Although, she probably knew already. Before I put my phone away, I sent a text to Sage.

Go to the church tonight if you want. I'm looking into a new lead.

As we exited off the freeway I got a response.

Fine. Meet up in a few hours then?

I sent her a yes and shoved my phone in my pocket. Gabriel's eyes glanced up at me from the rearview mirror. I'm not sure if he cared I had been on my phone, but he did work for the Primus and that was reason enough to be a little on edge. I stared at his reflection, which gave a little smile, and suddenly I trusted him completely.

We pulled into an empty parking lot behind the West Gate Bank. It was a seriously impressive building. Indissoluble, yet timeworn brick boasted itself to all passerby, standing three stories tall, with high windows and a balcony wrapping around the third floor. Small windows jutted out from the roof like miniature steeples.

In a flash, Gabriel hopped out of the vehicle and opened the door for me—what a gentleman—and I stepped out onto the crumbling asphalt.

"Follow me," he said, plucking a ring of keys from his pocket.

He stopped at the back door, unlocked it, and motioned me inside. He escorted me down a narrow hallway to an elevator. He faced the doors as they slid shut and casually pressed the button for the third floor. I felt a subtle jerk as we were carried up, and when the doors squeaked open he led me down another corridor, stopping at the last door on the right. He knocked three times, a steady and controlled knock, illustrating a practiced and perfected execution. It was a simple notion, but I found it admirable as it showed how disciplined he was. But this was also a bit intimidating.

The door swung open revealing a pinstripe suit. My gaze climbed up toward its face and then flinched back in horror. The man's eyelids were sewn shut and infected along the fusing skin.

A hideous grin broke on his face and lingered there. He held out his arm, welcoming me inside.

"Please, have a seat," he said, still grinning. "Master will be with you shortly."

The door clicked shut behind me; Gabriel had not followed. And suddenly, I didn't feel safe.

The old brick outside the building was deceiving; the inside was luxurious and modern. A single window interrupted tall, beige walls with gold moulding. Deep mahogany chairs with ornately carved patterns sat around a matching coffee table in the center of the room. They were cushioned in crushed red velvet.

I sat down with a painful amount of care and looked to the far end of the room where a stone slab sat like a monument, all alone. I looked back toward the eyeless man and he seemed to be able to sense I was staring at him.

"Are you thirsty?"

He walked deftly to the back of the room and brought back a gleaming platter, a golden goblet placed directly in the center. He bowed, offering it to me. I didn't need to look to know it was blood in the goblet. I took the goblet and that mad grin showed itself again.

"Freshly embalmed this morning."

My eyes flashed to the stone slab and a chill crawled up my spine. This was a mistake. I shouldn't have come here. The trust I felt with Gabriel had vanished. A queasiness squirmed inside me as the butler walked through a door in the back of the room. And then I waited in fear, dread, regretting the decision I made to come here. I had the sudden urge to get up and leave, to jump out a window if I had to. I set down the goblet and got ready to run, when I heard the quiet creak of the door opening.

My head snapped around to the corner and a tall woman with fiery red curls walked into the room. She wore a long, black dress that flowed ephemerally and had a slit down the side that revealed sculpted calves. Behind her walked in a stout and brutish man with a thick neck and shoulders. Following him was another man, yet, who wore a navy blue suit and whose jawline the gods themselves must've sculpted.

He glanced at me, expressionless. All color was drained from one eye and the other appeared to be nothing but an enlarged pupil.

I waited nervously for something to happen as they stood in a line, facing me. I didn't think I should be the first to speak. I didn't know what to say anyway. I didn't know why I was there.

But then another set of footsteps sounded from the doorway and a tall man strode in, well over six foot. He wore a three-piece suit, the long coattail flapping with each step. His jet-black hair was slicked back with not a strand out of place.

He turned towards me, his near translucent hands folded in front of him and blood red eyes studying me meticulously.

"Welcome, Maaria," he said. His voice was deep and commanding.

And I could do nothing but stare at him, afraid to speak.

"As I am sure you have assumed, I am Serafino. And I am the head," he swept his hand through the air, acknowledging the others, "of this Regency. My right hand and second in command," he indicated the handsome and daunting man with the mismatched eyes, "Dario. Our assertive—but otherwise useless—muscle, Damon. And our whore," he smirked, "Drusilla."

None of them gave the slightest response to being addressed.

"And of course, you have already met Gabriel, our harbinger."

I nodded dumbly.

"You can relax, Maaria. You have chosen to be here, and as you should know, this means you are considered an ally. A friend. Besides, you would not have been summoned at all if I hadn't thought you to be of some worth."

Whatever nerve I had left crumbled with each successive word. It was as if his articulated speech somehow drained me of my composure and he absorbed it for himself. Each second, he became a more imperturbable force. And I became a void of terror.

"Let me get straight to the point," he said, his shoulders broadening. "We know who you are. We know what you are doing. We know you are aware of the Ring of Solomon and that you wish to retrieve it. And I must assume you know that our race is an endangered species. I am curious, Maaria, why do you think the Primus wants the ring?"

My eyes widened and I felt the strange boiling sensation of panic. And the more it boiled, the more bubbles of fear rose to the surface of consciousness, trapping me there. Serafino raised an eyebrow at me, waiting.

My lips struggled to form the word, but I sputtered out, "P—Power?"

I caught a quivering in the red lips of Drusilla. She offered a sardonic grin as I glanced at her.

"Yes, there is an obvious power in the ring. But it is precisely this power the ring holds which will revive our species. You see, Maaria, the Primus is the ruler over all remaining members of the Nobilis Sanguis, and it is our duty as the vampiric government to obey him and return our race to its former glory. And it is us, the undead, who own the inherent right to this world, not mortals. With the Ring of Solomon, we could, quite literally, rule the world.

"So I have summoned you here tonight, Maaria, to ask you to assist us. Believe me when I say I have taken notice of your ambition, and it could prove to be indispensable. And it is my honor to ask you to join our efforts in unearthing the ring."

He paused.

I knew I couldn't say no, for fear of being killed or worse, but I couldn't bring myself to say yes either.

In a petty effort to stall, I said, "Why me? I'm not a...a Valde."

"Ah, yes," he said. "The Nobilis Sanguis may only accept members of the Royal Blood, all of which are members of the Valde race, but the Primus has given me the duty of selecting members for this Regency without any restriction of race. I can recruit any Awakened, so long as they show value and willingness to serve our objectives. This Regency may be hired by the Primus, but it operates outside the confines of the Nobilis Sanguis."

That explained why they had the Lussuro, Gabriel, working for them. I assumed Drusilla was also a Lussuro, and that the other was a Beznabala, brutish as he was.

I nodded. "And what do I get out of this, other than betraying my friends?" I instantly regretted saying it, but Serafino only pursed his thin lips.

"You may be betraying your friends, but it is for the greater good. It is necessary to bring Awakened a rule over mortals. Imagine a world, Maaria, where you no longer have to hide, where everything is beneath you. And if you agree to help us, you will be among the most praised. The rewards will be beyond your wildest dreams.

"You will never have to hunt for food again. You will be feared and respected. You will be rich. You will learn abilities you never dreamed existed. You will be amongst the most deified and exalted vampires in history."

He made it sound so enticing, but I didn't believe a word he said. The last of my trust had walked out the door with Gabriel. But, having recovered some of my confidence, I said, "What is it exactly, that you want me to do?"

A satisfied grin showed on his face, but it was still measured and artificial, making him all the more predatory and dangerous. A snake.

"We take our orders directly from the Primus. His immense age has fogged his memory, but during his lucid episodes he will recall details he has otherwise forgotten. We discover information as he does, for we cannot act without his orders.

"It will be your job to do the rest. You will keep our opposition in line and make certain that they do not make any advantageous moves over us. You will lead them astray if need be and be required to do whatever we ask of you. And should you agree to do this, I pray you do not try to double-cross us. I can absolutely guarantee you it would only end in fatality. Of course, you will be summoned here regularly and anything you do outside these walls will be made known to us. You can count on that." He paused. And then, "What do you say, Maaria?"

If he was bluffing, I couldn't tell. But I didn't see an option either way. Say no, I die. I was reluctant to say it but I did:

"I'll do it."

THE BUTLER DIRECTED ME DOWNSTAIRS AND Gabriel stood outside the elevator doors, waiting to drive me back. After the Escalade peeled away from my shed and I was free from any peering eyes, I called Sage, who picked up almost immediately.

"Jesus, Maaria. I've been waiting."

"There's a…a few hours until sunrise. Want to go for a quick hunt in the woods?"

Silence.

"Okay. I'll meet you in fifteen."

She hung up. As I awaited her arrival, the gravity of what had just transpired settled in. Slowly at first, and then all at once, like the bank itself had collapsed on top of me. I was lost. I had no idea what I was going to do, how I was going to maneuver all this. And I definitely had no idea how I was going to tell Sage. But I had to.

Someone had to play the role of the hero. Someone had to save us all—I didn't believe Serafino's bullshit story about saving our race or taking over the world. And no one had applied for the hero position, so I took it for myself.

No matter how necessary that decision was it is one that I will forever regret, even though I never really had a choice in the matter. It was do it or die. That's how this existence works.

I spotted Sage walking up the road and I pulled my hood up and went out to meet her. We turned in unison to walk across the street and into the trees.

"Did you find anything?" I asked her.

She shook her head. "Nothing. I searched through everything. There's no evidence a ring is there or ever has been. What's this new lead?"

"Um...it's not exactly a lead, per say. And it's risky, but I uh, I think it could pay off."

"Okay?" she said. "What is it?"

"I met with this—they—they call themselves a Regency. They're hired by—"

"You what?"

"I met—"

"You met with the Regency? What the *hell* were you thinking, Maaria?" She stopped me and grabbed my arm, her eyes searing into mine with white-hot fury.

Caught you. Guilty. No plea bargain available.

"You know about the Regency? You never told me about a Regency."

She shook her head; fast little shakes that sent her face backward into her neck like turtle. She was on the defensive now.

"I never had a reason to tell you," she said.

I shook my arm from her grip. "You can quit keeping secrets now. I mean, goddamn it, if you ever want to find this ring, then I'm sorry, but we have to work together."

"What are you talking about? We are working together," she said.

"Are we? Because we haven't really gotten much work done. You can't keep anything like this from me. Just because I'm not as old or experienced as you doesn't mean I'm useless. They summoned *me* there, not you."

"Yeah, because you're young and naive," she spat.

"If I was naive as they thought me to be, I would've believed him—but I don't. And I want to use them to our advantage. Or at least try."

She fell silent. The trees closed in on us with every step and dying leaves fell as the wind gently carried them to the ground. She must have found the same comfort in the trees as I always have, because I watched as her eyes followed the falling leaves and the hard edge in them gradually softened.

"What happened?" she said.

So I told her everything. About Gabriel, the West Gate Bank that was operated by vampires, the Regency, the butler with no eyes, the Primus and his 'lucid episodes,' the stone slab used to bleed out mortals, and Serafino's offer to me if I were to help them find the Ring.

Sage might still try to keep secrets, but I knew that the time for secrets was over. If we wanted even a chance at beating these guys, the games needed to end. Only after we save our race from those lunatics could we amuse ourselves with frivolous schemes again.

Sage was silent for a moment after I told her.

"I couldn't say no," I said. "They would've killed me. Maybe I can get information out of them, you know?"

"What information? They don't have any or they wouldn't be asking for your help. This means we're ahead of them. They're afraid."

"Maybe," I said. "How long can we stay ahead of them, though? He said anything I do outside those walls will be made known to them. How are we supposed to keep out of their sight?"

"An empty threat, maybe." She paused. "You said they'll summon you there regularly. Why would they need to do that if they're watching your every move already?"

"Valid. We'll just need to move fast."

"I don't like this, Maaria. Believe me. It was stupid of you. You're so young; they're using you, playing games with you. They're delusional, yeah, but they're not dumb. They know how to manipulate people. And what if this is all for nothing? What if there is no ring in the first place? He said the Primus has 'ludic episodes?' What the fuck does that mean? Doesn't sound very credible. He's probably pulling all this ring talk out of his ass."

"I don't know. He said he's really old. His immense age—those were his exact words. Mornor told me that can happen as you get older. Your memory kind of fogs over."

"Yeah it can happen, but it's not a natural thing. It's what happens when you're a deranged lunatic.

You get addicted to vampire blood, you start drinking them dry. Like dry as dust dry. You following? You go mad. The guy's a little off his rocker. It's hard to know how much of what the guy says is actually credible.

"But you're right. No more secrets. You'll need my help. You can't handle all them on your own, it's too dangerous. You shouldn't have gone at all."

"They didn't really give me a choice, Sage. Either way—"

Sage's elbow slammed into my stomach and cut me off.

"What?" I hissed.

She pressed a finger to her lips and silently drew the machete from her waist. Her lips barely moved when she whispered, "Did you hear that?"

"Hear what?"

A branch snapped to our left. Both of our heads snapped in its direction.

"Our meal?" I chuckled softly.

She turned and glared at me. She took a few careful steps toward the sound when the thing shot through the trees, a dimly glowing pair of eyes growing steadily larger until a wolf jumped out of the brush and bared its fangs, aiming right for her.

Her blade swung through the air, missing the wolf, and it tackled her to the ground. I ran to her and drew my gun. The wolf's eyes locked into mine and it growled menacingly. The gun shook in my hands. I don't know why I was so scared by it, it was just an animal and an animal's only reason for existence now was to keep me alive. But I was scared and felt threatened. The way its eyes transmitted its message felt all wrong. It was like they spoke and said: This is my business, now back off and let me take care of it.

Sage's arm clambered through the fallen leaves, desperately reaching for the cold touch of her blade. It was useless. I saw the machete fly from her hands and into some bushes when the wolf threw itself against her.

She looked at me helplessly, eyes full of fear. The animal's paws still placed firmly on her chest as she lay there beneath its snapping jaws. I think it was the rare glimpse of vulnerability in Sage that made me freeze.

"Shoot it!" she yelled.

I curled my shaking finger around the trigger, but the wolf jumped off Sage and bounded toward me. I waited a second too long to pull the trigger. The animal ran into me and knocked me over. Teeth tore into my arm and the smell of my own blood filled my nostrils before I saw it pouring out of my arm. The gun was nowhere in sight.

The wolf's attention snapped back to Sage. The adrenalin of pain made up for the clarity I lost with the loss of blood. I saw her standing up, machete in hand once more. She swiveled the blade around and the wolf left me to lie there, bleeding.

It crouched low and snarled at her. It began to circle her, preparing for a fight.

On hands and knees, I scrambled for my gun. When my hand wrapped around it, I stood up and faced them. Sage was grinning. She was thrilled. And this was her fight. So I stood there, arm limp at my side, and the blood dripping down onto the gun in my hand.

They circled each other slowly. I watched half warily, half amused. Then they stopped. Sage's back was to me, the wolf facing me. But its attention didn't stray from the girl swinging the blade. It lurched forward and I raised my gun, ready to shoot in case of trouble.

But the wolf's body morphed as it leapt through the air. Like a tadpole, its legs seemed to grow longer. Its snout shorter. And then the thing landed on its feet, barely a yard from Sage.

It was a man.

I stepped forward and aimed my gun at him.

And then a strange sound emanated from Sage, like she was choking back tears.

And she cried out, "Ralph?"

Chapter Eleven

M Y EYES DARTED BETWEEN THEM, hands still clutching the gun which shook even worse than before. They just stared at each other like I wasn't even there. Sage's mouth hung open in disbelief and the other's mouth warped in bittersweet triumph. The silence boomed with anticipation. I couldn't bear it. Still aiming the gun at him, I stepped forward. Somebody had to say something. Break the silence.

"Don't shoot," Sage whipped around to face me. A stern expression was set on her face, entirely non-malleable, like clay sent through the kiln. "Put the gun down. Maaria."

I slowly lowered the gun and her full attention returned to this man before us.

"Ralph," she said wistfully, looking at him like he was some long lost lover from another life.

He gave a chuckle that was choked off by emotion. "That's me," he said.

His nose was snout-like and his ears barely protruded from beneath wavy auburn hair. They were set higher on his scalp than they should have been. His jaw was full of stubble and he wore a tan cargo jacket. Everything about him seemed wolf-like. A werewolf?

I checked his aura. Pale. Pink-white.

He was a vampire.

And then it all came rushing in. Ralph. Ralph. I knew the name. Sage's brother. Her mortal brother. The one who had lived in Chicago with her, who wanted her to come home for the Sarah Vaughn show. Was this her brother? But it couldn't be…

Sage's hand hovered over her mouth, all contorted with painful hesitation. But then she lurched forward and threw her arms around him. They wrapped violently around Ralph's muscular build and he did the same. Locked in a fervent embrace, his arms ventured up her back and stroked her hair.

It was so human. So filled with genuine emotion.

He pulled away from her, resting a hand on either side of her face, tenderly cupping her jaw. And he began to laugh. The warmest smile beamed on his face and revealed a set of pearlescent fangs.

Together, they stood there for what seemed like hours. Smiling and laughing, holding each other. Not saying a word. Dim moonlight cast a surreal glow about them, illuminating their private reverie with a preciousness I couldn't deny. It was cinematic as hell.

And I stood, arrested by this rapturous impossibility.

When at last they separated and collected awareness of the world around them once more, Sage turned to me, the crystalline pools of her eyes dancing under a film of tears. She was crying.

"Maaria, I have to go," she whispered.

I didn't respond, but she understood.

And as she turned away, she disappeared from sight. And the man named Ralph followed her, shifting from man to wolf in mid-stride.

THE NEXT NIGHT I RECEIVED A TEXT FROM Sage saying she was going to feed and asked me to meet up afterward. Without hesitation, I sent back a yes and went out on the fringes of town to feed on my own.

When I returned to my shed, I remembered I'd told Annabelle I would meet with her tonight. I thought about letting Sage know I couldn't be out late, but didn't want to raise any suspicions. I guess I was the one keeping secrets now. Oops.

Minutes later, I heard the soft crunch of two pairs of feet trampling the withered leaves outside.

"You must know who this is, Maaria." She grabbed his hand and they stood there in my doorway and I felt like a parent being asked for my daughter's approval of her new boyfriend. But that scenario couldn't be farther from the truth.

"Your brother? Your mortal brother."

Sparks flashed in her eyes at the mention of the word brother.

"Yes," she said.

"But how?"

She looked to Ralph. He shrugged.

"You know her story," he said. "She never came home. Gone. Disappeared. And I had waited. Missed the show, in the desperate hopes she would return. But she didn't. So I waited for the call from my family. I dreaded that moment, but what I dreaded more was never knowing where she was. And then the call came and they told me she had been kidnapped."

He made his way to the desk chair and sat down. Sage and I sat across from him on the end of my makeshift bed.

"I couldn't believe it. She had survived and thrived amongst all the drug dealers in Chicago, but now she was kidnapped in a small town in northeast

Wisconsin? It didn't make sense. Weeks had passed and we all assumed the worst. They declared her dead and had a bodiless funeral. I didn't go. I couldn't bring myself to do it. I couldn't accept she was gone. I wouldn't believe it. I didn't want to mourn for something I didn't think was gone. That would make it too real, too final.

"So I left Chicago. I never liked it there much anyway," he gave a small, knowing smirk to Sage, "and I went to search for her. She had to be out there somewhere. I refused to believe she was gone. I needed her. I needed answers, something. I spent two years taking odd jobs, searching wherever I could for some sort of information, some clue to her presence. I found nothing.

"But then I went to a bar one night. There was this man there. He was strange, different. We had gone outside for a cigarette and...all the birds. They just seemed to stare at him. And he stared back at them, like he was silently communicating with them, and then they all flew away. All at once."

He started to lose himself in the past and I saw the vague haze of memory wash over his clear, amber eyes. Just the same as Sage.

"He was a vampire. I didn't know it at the time, but he was. I talked to him about my sister, about Sage, and what happened to her up near Green Bay. And I think that rang some bells. He must've known you, seen you somewhere, heard of you, something. Because he told me I would see her in another life. He was so sure of it. He said he could take me there. And then the fear hit me. I thought he was going to kill me. I mean he did, in a way. And the next thing I remember, I was in a cabin, dying. But my body was still alive.

"He stuck around for a day. Doesn't matter. That's not the important part of the story. But I left and went searching for Sage ever since then. My Sire vanished; I didn't know anyone. I was alone for decades. Just a tourist, passing through different towns, talking to every vampire I came across, asking to see if they knew anything about Sage. And then a few months ago, I came across this girl. Weird girl. There was something off about her. I don't know if it was madness or age, but she told me to go here. And now I've finally found you."

Sage gave a short smile. "Now I have a brother and a sister," she said.

Ralph furrowed his brows.

"Maaria. She's my sister in the blood. We share the same Sire," she explained. "But. We have more pressing matters to attend to. The ring. Let's go."

She led the way into town and Ralph and I followed. Reuniting with her brother had brought upon some internal change in her. She still had her fierceness, she always would, but it had calmed. There were no more abrupt throes of outrage. She was quieter, more reserved. I wasn't sure if I liked it yet. But I loved her all the same.

WE ARRIVED AT THE LIBRARY TO SEE THE window I had previously broken in through had been replaced. I wondered what they thought about the whole scenario. Someone broke into a library of all places. Not to mention I didn't even take anything.

We didn't have to break anything a second time, though. Ralph had had the sense to invest in a lock pick. We entered through a side door and went to the computers. Sage and I sat down and got online, in search of any information or lore about the Ring of Solomon. We knew now that the ring wasn't at the church and had no idea where it could be located, so our obvious next step was simply to learn more about it. Ralph wandered off in search of a Bible or any other religious, quasi-religious, sacred, or occult texts.

Sage and I searched the internet, but it didn't take long for her to get up and leave.

"I'm going to go help Ralph skim through books."

"Sounds good."

Once she'd gone, I took out my phone and sent a message to Annabelle.

I'll meet you in a few hours.

She didn't reply, but I assumed she got the message.

During the few short hours we spent in the library, we found a barrage of useless information and only a small sum that was of any use to us.

Ralph was easily the most organized vampire I have ever known. Like a mortal student or scholar, he always took notes. Always read things, like novels, newspapers, even the pointless ramblings of mortals on their blogs. He was resourceful in the most human way, more sensible than any Awakened. And this night was no exception.

We gathered around a table and Ralph stood before us with a little notebook clutched in his hands.

"Let's recap what we've found, I suppose. Or at least what's of any use to us," Ralph said, his snoutish nose buried in the pages of his leather notebook. "Solomon asked God for wisdom and he received it. He was rumored to be a magician and exorcist, and had seven hundred wives and three hundred concubines. The first mention of a ring is when a supposed archangel gave him a ring of bronze and iron with a special seal engraved on it. This ring gave him the ability to speak to animals, to command the elements, and power over demons and all other manner of supernatural creatures.

"The brass part was signed with commands to the good genie, and the iron half to the bad genie, evil beings. The symbol was that of a five-pointed star, or the Star of David, and on each of the four points, was set a jewel, each given to him by four separate angels. These gave him power over the elements. A ruby for fire, aquamarine for the wind, emerald for earth, and a sapphire for water.

"The ring was purportedly thrown into the ocean by the demon Asmodeus and swallowed by a fish, hence, disappearing from recorded history forever," he snapped his notebook shut. "So while that's all fine and great, very informative and interesting, it gives us no suggestion whatsoever as to where such a ring might be located at this point in time."

He sighed heavily and shook his head.

I couldn't help but smile slightly. It was easy to see the similarities between he and Sage, even in the absence of humanity. It brought a fluttering of strange emotion in me. At least it was strange then. I know what it is now. It was empathy. And I thought I'd kicked humanity to the curb. Quite the opposite.

That empathy was also mixed with felicitation and envy. I was happy for them and this intimate, familial connection they shared, but I envied it. That tinge of jealousy for something I never had, or couldn't remember having. And even though Sage and I were also family, it would never be like what she shared with Ralph.

That was the moment where I was inflicted with a melancholy I have never quite been able to shake off. Even now, decades after the fact, it resides in me, impacting a heavy weariness. And every night I wonder how much longer I will be able to endure it. But that is another story entirely.

"So where do we go from here," Sage said, breaking the silence.

"I haven't the slightest clue," said Ralph. "Perhaps we should sit on it for a day or so. Really assess what we know and find the next logical place to look for an answer. There could be something in all this, something that could potentially point us in the right direction. Maybe we just have to look harder."

"But this is all ancient, how could any of this possibly pertain to—"

"He could be right," I interjected. "It's worth a shot, right?" Besides, there's nothing more we can do now without studying it. So let's take some time to do that, and at the very least, we'll know the ring's history can be ruled out as a lead."

A frustrated huff sounded from Sage. "Alright. I don't want to accept that answer; the Regency worries me too much. Thank you, by the way, Maaria. But I suppose you two are right."

"We'll just take the rest of the night," Ralph said, trying to assuage her. "Maybe a few hours into tomorrow night. We'll meet with Maaria in two days at the very latest. But if we rush ourselves...Sage."

She was looking away from him. Frustrated. I could feel the anger rising in her. The Sage I knew had not disappeared with Ralph's return after all.

"Sage," he said again and she looked back to him, eyes glaring. "If we rush, get hasty, we don't stand a chance at beating this Regency."

"How much do you know about this?" I asked. He had only been here one night.

"Sage told me everything last night. I wasn't here when rumors of the ring surfaced and the Primus began his hunt, but I know enough about the Nobilis Sanguis to understand that they cannot possess this ring, whatever powers it may or may not hold."

He had me curious now.

"You know this from when you were in Chicago?"

"No, I was mortal then. The Nobilis Sanguis' headquarters were in Chicago at the time, but I was clueless to it. I'd traveled west of here, into the mountains, when I first heard of them. The things they were capable of, the things they'd done."

"What did they do? No one's ever told me." I gave Sage an annoyed look and she gave a playful smirk back.

"They're one of two vampiric political factions," said Ralph, watching our exchange with amusement. "Well, now they're the sole political faction. They utterly destroyed the other—the Republicae Moderna. They fought for democracy among us, which is the antithesis of what the Nobilis Sanguis wants. The Republicae pushed too hard and the Sanguis pushed back, killing all of them. There weren't many of them to begin with, but it was still an atrocity. I met one of them a few years ago, who told me what happened.

"The Republicae didn't deserve the massacre that met them, but the Nobilis Sanguis does. Step one is to keep this damned ring out of their hands. And step two is to dissolve whatever remains of them."

My curiosity bested me yet again. "So what remains of them? Did most of them die in the fight with the Republicae Moderna?"

"No," said Sage. "Not long after I returned here after my time with the Shrine, they planned an operation to take back our rightful place as superior to mortals. Or so the rumor has it. Whatever. I never really paid much attention to that shit. Someone on the inside rose in mutiny, abolished all their efforts, and left them in shambles. Whatever's left of them fled up here to Milwaukee. I'm sure there's more to the story, but I don't know it."

"Me neither," said Ralph. "I only know the girl I met had been taken prisoner by them after their fight with the Republicae and was still there with them when it all happened."

My phone vibrated in my pocket.

"What's that," Sage teased, though I had the suspicion her playful attitude was a cover for her contempt. "Do you have a little friend I don't know about?"

Yup. Contempt.

I tried to feign a reaction of confused irritation when I looked at the message, but I know Sage saw right through it.

"It's Annabelle," I said, confirming Sage's suspicions.

"Don't..." was all she said; the remainder of her sentence trailing off into silent accusations.

"Let her do what she has to," said Ralph.

That was the first time I ever felt true gratitude in this unlife. Ralph had a way about him. He gave me a real glimpse into what it meant to be human.

WE PARTED WAYS AND I OPENED THE message from Annabelle.

Hurry Maaria. I'll only wait here so long.

Fearful of what she might do if I didn't meet her, I ran faster than I'd ever run before. When I reached the campus, I spotted that black fog hovering under the roof of the gazebo, winding in and out of spindles. Two glowing yellow spheres materialized and the blackness dissipated. She was leaning against the railing, one leg bent, arms folded across her chest. I ran even faster.

"Well, well, well," she said. "It took you long enough." A menacing giggle bubbled up.

"I had other matters to attend to," I said. "And I think you'll be glad I did."

She uncrossed her arms. "Enlighten me."

"The ring," I said. "It's not in the church, don't waste your time looking—"

"That makes me think maybe it is in the church."

"It's not," I said. "We don't know where it might be, but...I know why they might be after it."

Annabelle's eyes lit up at the words. "Please, do tell."

I hesitated, not sure how much I should tell her. "The ring," I said, "according to the lore anyway, holds the power to control any and all supernatural creatures."

Instant regret. The wrong words. She said she wanted to keep the ring from the Regency, wanted it destroyed, but I didn't put lying beyond her moral capacity. And I didn't put it past her to want to keep it for herself.

Her yellow eyes swelled as they tore into me, the only thing I could see. "Who's the boy?" she asked.

I stuttered, "He's…he's a friend. He shares our motives. He wants the ring gone, destroyed. And he's resourceful. So don't go thinking you can try and threaten him or something."

She looked taken aback. "I wouldn't dare." Her hellish giggle threatened to erupt again, dancing its way up and down her throat. "So long as I'm not threatened, I will not threaten any of your precious little friends. As long as you," she poked a finger at me, "continue to help me."

"Why do you even want my help? If we're truly after the same thing, why don't you just let us take care of it?"

"Because!" she shouted. "That little bitch refuses to work with me, work together for a common goal. And quite frankly, Maaria, I find that very irksome. If she would just swallow her ugly, goddamn pride, then maybe, just maybe, I wouldn't have to force you into a corner, working with me behind her back."

My curiosity screamed at me, dying to know what it was that caused her to hate Sage with such violence. But I knew better than to ask. I inhaled, beating those burning questions from my throat and back down into my lungs. And when I exhaled, they vanished—floating mutely along with the currents of the wind.

"Fine," I said. "I'll continue to help you. But know that it's only because I know I don't have any other choice."

She leaned toward me and shoved her jagged nail into her scalp. A single drop of blood trickled down the end of her hair, where it pooled, wavering dangerously, threatening to fall to the ground.

"Oh, trust me," she said, "I know."

The drop of blood fell, forming a single red, juxtaposing splash on the white boards beneath us.

"You know," she sneered, "if you're trying to dig deeper into what you know about the ring, you might try going to St. Catherine's."

My head tilted in confusion.

"It's the oldest church in the area," she explained. "And I hear it has one hell of a library."

"…Umm, thanks," I said.

She giggled and licked her fangs. "You're welcome. I trust you'll keep me informed after I just seriously helped you out here." She twisted her ring and as the fog engulfed her, she walked away.

Chapter Twelve

I WANDERED OFF TO ST. CATHERINE'S AS soon as I woke the next night. I didn't inform anyone and I didn't feed; I was on a mission. And I was determined to find some answers. The church was pretty far out of town—just outside the suburbs north of Milwaukee—and it took me close to an hour to get there.

All the doors were locked, but fortunately, I was able to find a window that was open just a crack. I breathed a small sigh of relief knowing I wasn't going to have to break another window.

It's not that it bothered me, really. I just didn't want to make a habit of it. Didn't want to take the slightest risk of letting mortals catch on. Not that they would make any connection between a broken library window and a church window that was a fifteen minute drive away, but I still felt like I should be

160

careful. I should be more worried about the Regency taking notice of it, rather than mortals. But then, did it really make any difference to the Regency whether a window was broken or not? I didn't know what kind of attention they paid to detail, or if they were even watching me at all.

But more importantly, I had to ask myself: Did it matter? Did it matter if they were watching me? I mean, if I weren't willing to take any risks, they would win. If I played it too safe, they would kill me off for not helping to further their efforts and would find someone else to take my place. And that someone could easily be someone more naive or someone who was completely complacent to their desires. I absolutely could not take that gamble.

I scuffled through the church, opening doors and slamming them shut, looking for the library Annabelle said would be here. I found a set of stairs and traipsed down them. The walls were old and a musty smell wafted up from the basement.

I set foot into the underground room and flipped on a light. Shelves upon shelves of old documents and books, Bibles of every translation and volume scattered everywhere. Richly varnished tables spaced between the shelves, each furnished with a small lamp. And each of them had a thin drawer hiding under the smooth lip of the tabletop. I opened one of them. Notebooks, parchment, pens, highlighters, even quills.

My first thought was that Ralph would love it here. But wouldn't I? I had been a writer as a mortal, or so Mornor had told me. Why didn't this room stir some bittersweet nostalgia in me? I realized I truly wished it had. I wanted to feel the coziness the scent of worn and handled pages provided, the enchanting spirit of history, the wistful ambience. But I felt nothing.

I didn't have time to dwell on these things. I had work to do. A vast collection of literature was waiting for me to wade through it.

I searched for hours. Any title that caught my attention that looked to relate in the slightest to what we were looking for—what we knew—I read it. I searched with a diligence I didn't know I had. Most everything I found was just a reiteration of what we already knew. Perhaps more detailed, a slightly different translation or interpretation, but essentially the same.

I held an ancient book. It told of pre-Biblical myths, how they came to be what they are now. How their history had changed since the oral stories began to the time they were scribed into text. Blueprints for Noah's ark, the Sumerian Edin, the Lamp of Constantine, Solomon's Seal, the Nephilim, the Gospel of Judas was there too, and many others.

The chords in my neck stood out and my jaw was clenched as I flipped through endless pages, feeling like I was wasting my time.

And that's when I felt it. I'd been flipping past pages so fast that I had passed it, but there was a page that felt different. Thicker than all the others. My hand hovered over the pages. It's nothing, I thought, just a few pages stuck together with age. It was a really old book—centuries old at least.

Whatever. It didn't matter how old the book was. What mattered was that odd page. It stuck out among all the useless shit I'd flipped through. But now, logic told me it had to be pages fused together by the substance of past. It was the only thing that made sense. My hand still dangled there, waiting for the synapses in my brain to tell it what to do—flip back or flip forward. The hell with it. I'll take anything I can get right now.

So I flipped back. Found the page.

And there it was. Nestled right into the spine, edges curling gently away from the page it was stuck to. A blank sheet of parchment. It was thicker, looked younger than the rest of the book. I flipped to the other side of the page it was stuck to and right at the top it read: *The Lore of the Seal of Solomon.*

My hand was shaking. Whether with excitement or trepidation, it was impossible to tell. The room around me disappeared. The only things in existence were myself, the book with the displaced parchment, and the foreboding current that flowed in-between— enveloping me entirely, binding me tightly, choking all sense of self and reality from me until it burst violently outward and left me entirely. My hand shot forward like it was possessed and it woke me from my trance. Silently, I counted to three and gathered my wits.

I peeled the parchment back away from the page as carefully as I could and turned it over. I didn't know what it was, but I knew it was of utmost significance. A message. Surely placed here on purpose for someone to find. This was paramount. A colossal discovery of burning import. This is what we were looking for, what we needed. It was pivotal.

And I couldn't look away from it.

IV

α τομβ, α ρινγ, α χιλδ. Ι
φωργεδ μανσ ανθεμσ. σεαρχ θε
ωλδ πλασε—λωρε,
   ιτσ ενδινγ. θισ τομβ, ι φινδ,
   ιτ ρησιδσ.

-R.B.C.B.

The only thing I understood was the insignia penned at the top—Solomon's Seal. The very seal that was supposedly etched on the Ring of Solomon. Whoever brought the ring here had written this with the intention of it being found. But why? Wasn't the point to keep it away from everyone?

There was a loud scraping sound of a chair being pushed back and I found myself standing up with a terrifying thought:

Morning.

How long had I been here? Hours. I had no idea how many. There were no windows or clocks. I panicked. I couldn't be trapped down here all day. If someone found me, I'd be helpless, comatose in a sunlight slumber.

I picked up the parchment, carefully rolled it up and put it in my sweatshirt pocket, taking the ancient book back to its place on the shelves. I flipped off the lights as I bounded up the stairs, taking them three at a time.

Darkness.

Only two hours of precious twilight until the deadly rays of the dawn. I ran. Ran faster and faster until I didn't know if my feet could carry me any quicker. I pulled out my phone and dialed Sage's number.

"Hello."

"Sage," I gasped. "Where are you?"

"Are you okay?" She said, sounding half concerned, half mocking.

"It's important," I said.

"I'm at my place."

"Where is it?"

No answer.

"Sage, where is it? Please."

I POUNDED ON THE DOOR. THIRST GNAWED AT me, but it would have to wait—just like I had to wait for Sage to let me inside. I was outside a small cabin in the woods. I had never been this way before. A light shone through the planks in the window and I knew she was inside. I was just about to knock again when the door flew open. Ralph stood in front of me, taken aback by my appearance. I must have looked hysterical. He stepped back and let me inside. It was a small place, but cozy. Nicely furnished and full of human charm. It felt like a home. Or at least what I thought a home should feel like. There was a table on one wall and I whipped the parchment out from my pocket and slammed it on the table.

"Look," I breathed. "Look what I found."

The two of them crowded around me at the table, leaning over me to see what it was I was so frantic over.

"What the hell is that?" asked Sage.

Ralph leaned in further—eyes squinting and brow crumpled together in an accordion furrow—and studied the symbols. "A message?" he said.

I nodded. "Yeah, and look at that." I pointed to the symbol and Ralph looked up at me with a glorious revelation gleaming in his eyes.

"The Seal of Solomon." He looked at Sage.

"Where did you find it?" she said.

"In the library of this old Catholic church outside town. It was…it was inside a book."

Sage's scrutinizing gaze fell on me. She was suspicious; if she didn't already know it was Annabelle's idea. But she couldn't be mad. She had no right to be angry. It paid off, didn't it? Ralph walked off, peering through the thin crack in the boarded up windows.

"The sun's going to rise soon, Maaria. You should get going. Bring this over at dusk. We should start trying to decode it right away. See if it's even useful."

I could make out the treeline, my shed standing a road's width away, when the sun's rays began to trickle over the horizon. Their warmth blushed my skin. The road was in sight. I tried to run faster, but the light made me hot and tense. I felt like I was going to turn to stone and burst into flame all at the same time.

My mind was frenzied, and when I made it to the road—without protection from the trees—pure adrenalin and survivalism pulled me across the pavement.

Steam rose off my skin and it started to sizzle. I had no thoughts; I barely even registered what was happening. I just ran, filled with excruciating pain. And as soon as I crashed through the door, I fell to the ground, wheezing and convulsing until the darkness of the room cooled my skin and the call of sleep consumed me.

I WAS BACK AT THE CABIN AND THE PARCH-ment sat back on the table. We pored over it. We had to. If we wanted to survive, we needed to decipher this. Because if the Regency beat us to the ring we would never survive, or at least not with any semblance of freedom. I didn't care what Serafino told me about promises of grandeur and wealth. It was all lies. Even if it wasn't—I didn't want any of it. Not from him.

We spent nights researching, studying Greek dictionaries, all in an attempt to translate this message. And here we sat again.

"It doesn't mean anything," Ralph said finally.

"What do you mean it doesn't mean anything?" said Sage.

"It doesn't mean anything," he repeated. "These words. They're not even words. They don't exist anywhere in the Greek language. They mean nothing."

Dejected and confused, we parted ways and I went back to my shed. The more I thought, the more it didn't make any sense. This was far too coincidental and seemingly premeditated to be meaningless. I couldn't help myself from thinking this was some sort of auspicious sign, that I was meant to find this, that it was meant to guide us to victory.

That morning, when I went to sleep, I was thrust into a strange and feverish dream. Strobing and thrashing between erratic flashes of color and thought, and periods of darkness and panic. Filled with tremors and cold sweats. But when I awoke I knew. So suddenly I knew; a rush of clarity surging within me.

Whoever placed this message in the book had left it to be found. But that was just it. It wasn't a message at all. It was a code. If this message was about the ring—which I could only assume it was—they would not have made it so easy as a simple translation to solve.

I grabbed my phone and dialed Sage's number. Each ring seemed to draw out for minutes in my anticipation. The fifth ring was cut short and before she had to time speak I blurted out:

"It's a code."

XIII

Chapter Thirteen

AND THERE WE WERE AGAIN. IN THE same cabin, huddled around the same table, the same enigmatic parchment in front of us. We knew now it was a code, but had no idea how to go about solving it. We constantly bickered over it and the environment got more and more tense as the night went on.

"Maybe it's just the letters," I blurted out.

Sage looked at me, perplexed.

"They're not Greek words," I said. "Ralph checked it time and time again, so maybe it's just the letters. We just translate each letter to its English equivalent."

Ralph pulled up a chair, grabbed his pen, and hunched over it. We waited as he scribbled, his hair whipping back and forth as he looked from his notes to the parchment. He let out a short laugh. "You were right."

We jumped to attention as he turned toward us and read.

"A tomb, a ring, a child. I forged man's anthems. Search the old place, lore, its ending. This tomb, I find, it resides."

Silence.

"So it's a riddle?" said Sage.

"There's a few spelling errors where translations aren't direct," he said. "Some of the letters had to be substituted. There's an *E* missing in resides, if that means anything. It says 'resids.'"

"Let me see," Sage demanded, pulling the parchment with his translation toward her.

And it read:

A tomb, a ring, a child. I phorged mans anthems. Search the old plase—lore, its ending. This tomb, I phind, it resids.

It all seemed too careful, too deliberate, for all those little mistakes. For a letter to be so carelessly forgotten.

"What does it mean?" I asked.

"Well," said Ralph, "the first part here seems biographical. Like a 'hey, this is who I am.' It's only the second half of it that seems to address the ring's actual location. If that's what it's suggesting at all."

"Search the old place, lore…" Sage mumbled. "So it resides in the tomb of where…what? Where the lore's ending says it is?"

Ralph laughed. "Yeah, well according to that logic, it's in the ocean somewhere, swallowed by a fish that's dead, that decayed millennia ago. So obviously that's either a lie, some way for mortals to rationalize an incomprehensible truth, or it's just plain ignorance."

"Not to mention, according to the lore, it was thrown into the sea on the other side of the globe."

"You were right about one thing, Sage. It's no answer, only another riddle."

"So if whoever wrote this is leaving some clue about who he or she is," I said, "does that mean they're alive? Do they want us to find them?"

"Who knows?"

"Okay, let's think this through," said Ralph. "A tomb, a ring, a child. A ring—obviously the Ring of Solomon. I think we can all agree on that. A tomb—most likely the same tomb referred to in the lore. So, the ocean. A child—no idea what that means. I forged mans—"

"Wait," I said. "Annabelle was the one who told me about all this. She said whoever brought the ring was part of a lineage who has guarded it for centuries. So maybe it means, like Child, you know? The Child of his Sire before him."

"Makes sense. Now, I forged man's anthems. What anthems? And of man, literally, or of Awakened?"

"Probably man," said Sage. "You said it yourself, the lore is probably some mortal fabrication. They're singing the anthems of this person's lies."

"What about the missing letter?" I asked. "Why do it? I don't think it was a mistake. Impossible. It's so meticulously structured. The way it's put together, there's just no way it was an accident."

But it was all too much to take in, so we went out together and fed to try and clear our heads. With each progression we made toward solving this riddle, it seemed to become only more puzzling.

Even after I left the cabin and retreated to my own little haven, I could think of nothing but this message. However hard I tried to bring my attention elsewhere, my mind always wandered back to it. To that missing *E*. I was obsessed with it. There had to be a meaning for it, and I refused to believe otherwise.

WE SCOURED THE LIBRARY BELOW THE OLD St. Catherine's church for clues the next night. And the night after that we did the same thing to the little old church right here in town—St. James Lutheran. The church that started it all.

We searched for hours, for anything at all that could possibly point us in the right direction. And all the while, that missing *E* nagged at me, whispering in my ear and tugging at my sleeve. Begging me to pay more attention to it.

We found nothing of course. Someone put a lot of effort into keeping this ring hidden. Which made it all the more strange that someone put the effort into creating this message in the first place. It was nonsensical. Regardless of the causes, this ring was obviously not meant to be found easily. There wouldn't be clues lying around all over the place, no giant arrows to point us in the right direction. This parchment was likely the only thing anyone would ever have in order to solve this great mystery.

Frustrated, we returned to the cabin.

During the days spent researching, the atmosphere was tense more often than not. Sage and I came across Annabelle once, very briefly. We had just fed together and her fog slithered across the road ahead of us.

"Anything I should know?" she asked.

"No...no nothing," I said.

"Uh huh. And what's the message?"

"Fuck off," said Sage. "Nobody's helping you okay, just fuck off."

"Oh, that's right. I forgot. You're the stupid bitch who won't work together for the common good. Have you deci—"

"Oh, right, like you're fighting for the common good."

"Deciphered this message yet?" She smiled patiently.

"No," I said.

"Let me see it, then."

Sage laughed. "Absolutely not. No. We got this, don't worry about it."

Annabelle didn't reply, just glared at us and disappeared.

Even though the atmosphere was tense, it was also during this time that Sage, Ralph, and I became closer—truly became three undead siblings. We found a deep sense of family in one another. We laughed, we reminisced (or Sage and Ralph did), we talked of Mornor and other vampires they had met, we discussed our nature, our favorite taste in blood. We were almost human.

We were sometimes intellectual and philosophical in the gravest of ways, and other times we were playful with one another. There was a night where we wrestled in the woods together. Sage and I teamed up against Ralph in his feral canine form. Another night where Ralph facetiously asked us about two murder-suicides he read about in the paper shortly before he came here. He wondered if it was us, and if it was really a murder-suicide or a double-homicide. We laughed at that one. Murder was surprisingly easy to get away with when you're a vampire.

But tonight was a quiet night and Ralph sat on a cushioned armchair, newspaper in hand. Sage and I had left him to go out into the trees. We were attempting to catch a bat because Sage had been insistent about teaching me another Shrine ritual. She jumped up onto a tree, wrapping her slender arms around it and clinging to its rough bark. She climbed it expertly. At times, she was almost as animal as Ralph was.

Light poured through the gaps of the trees. I looked over to see Ralph standing in the doorway, newspaper still tightly gripped in his hands.

"Hey, what do you think of this," he shouted. "There was a recent grave mutilation at a cemetery in town. Does that kind of thing happen often around here, Sage? I assume not."

She jumped down from the tree, landing firmly on her feet. I envied her agility. I had skills much greater than a mortal, but they were nothing compared to her.

"No..." she said. "An upper class, fundamentalist Christian neighborhood with a grave mutilation? That doesn't happen. Ever. You think it could mean something to us, though?"

He chuckled. "Anything out of the ordinary is enough to mean something to me."

We walked to the cemetery. The moonlight shone down upon us in chrome and pewter hues, broken into fragments by the crooked branches of trees. It wrapped us in a rapturous atmosphere of both a feverish lunacy and a whimsical delight. Ralph was paces ahead of us with a bounce in his step. Sage walked next to me with her fist clenched around an invisible shovel. Tomorrow's newspaper would read about a re-mutilated grave. We left the shelter of the trees and further up the road were a smattering of headstones. Some were new and robust monuments while others were old and crumbling.

"Do you know what grave it is?" said Sage.

Ralph shook his head, his mane of auburn hair shimmering under the moonlight, becoming home to a thousand stars.

We trudged through the hoard of headstones, looking for signs of disturbed earth. After an hour, things started to look hopeless.

"Hey!" Ralph called out.

Sage and I hurried over. He pointed to the ground where clumps of dirt were mounded up unevenly. It looked like a recently dug burial site, but we were surrounded by graves nearly a hundred years old.

"Barth," he read from the headstone.

Sage and I looked at each other with mutual understanding. Barth. The old pastor of the church.

"Dig," I said.

And dig we did. What would have taken mortals hours, took us a mere twenty minutes. And when we heard the thud of the shovel hitting wood, we stopped, each looking back and forth to one another, waiting for someone to take the plunge and open the lid of the coffin. The only sound was the squeak of bats overhead.

I jumped down. I was loath to do it, but I heaved the lid open and peered inside. Shock. Confusion. Then a surge of exhilaration. And finally, more confusion. I looked up and Sage and Ralph were peering down at me.

And I simply said, "It's empty."

"What do you mean, it's empty?" Ralph asked.

I moved to let him look.

He gave Sage an inquisitive glance. She looked down at me, her blue eyes narrowed. "Maaria. Do you think he's a vampire?"

It had never occurred to me before, but it was the only thing that seemed to make sense. But why would he have roused himself from the grave, from whatever slumber he sought there? And why now? If he was, in fact, a vampire, was he an ally or another antagonist?

FUELED BY THE PREVIOUS NIGHT'S GRAVE discovery—pun intended—we met at my shed to make another attempt at discerning some meaning from the message on the parchment. We spent hours grasping at thin air, trying to find some meaning or reason for that conspicuous missing letter I had become so infatuated with. And once again, tensions were high.

"Okay, what's this then?" I asked, exasperated. "We have the initials and the insignia of Solomon's Seal, but why the Roman numerals? What's the significance in that? There has to be one. And four, why four?"

After minutes filled with nothing but silence, Ralph shot up from his chair.

"Every fourth letter." He got straight to work, counting them out. "Nothing," he said. He slid the paper over to us and it simply read: *micdodshscepeeenimhis*.

"How'd you do this?" I asked.

"What do you mean? I just took the original English transliteration and counted them out," he said.

"What if you correct all the grammar in it," offered Sage.

He scribbled again, yielding the same results: *micdrmaeehollingsbnrd.*

"Maybe this is something," he said, sounding like he was trying to fool himself into believing a reason where there was none. "If you look in the middle it says Dr. Mae E. Hollings…" He let the words drop off into a frustrated silence.

And there we were again, lost in our thoughts and back to the beginning. I gazed outside as the moon continued along its curving path around the sky. The temperature slowly began to rise and dewdrops glistened on the grass. I felt the shuffle of movement beside me as Sage and Ralph prepared to leave. The sun would be rising within the hour.

Desperate, I said, "Wait."

They stared expectantly back at me as I scrambled for a solution.

"The letters," I said, "the English equivalents. Some of them are two letters, but their Greek counterparts are only one, right?"

"Right…" said Ralph.

"So maybe…maybe those letters remain one letter when you count out every fourth. The phi, the chi, the theta. They're one letter." I could tell they weren't following me. "Dammit," I cried, "they're two separate messages, so solve them like two separate messages. Count out the letters from the Greek, then transcribe them!"

Ralph dashed past me and back to the desk, scribbling frantically. He looked up with wide eyes. "Michigan's rolling tides."

Sage looked bewildered. "Michigan's rolling...but."

"Lake Michigan," I said. "The lore. It says the ring was thrown into the ocean, swallowed by a fish. Maybe Lake Michigan represents the ocean. It's in the lake. Or near the lake."

She looked me dead in the eyes with her familiar look of fierce determination. "The campus."

They left just before the pink light of fire came roaring over the horizon. We wouldn't go to the campus just yet. We had no idea where we could begin to look and we didn't want to rouse suspicion from anyone. Not Annabelle, not the Regency, not from anyone else who might be watching. But we knew that this was it, this was the calm before the storm. Soon, others would find out about this. Soon there would be a war.

THE NEXT NIGHT I WENT TO THE CABIN AND we sat there in silence. Basking in the waning moments of solace, allowing ourselves to forget the impending crescendo of chaos. Ralph sat in the armchair, com-fortable and cool as ever. He looked quite like Mornor in all but appearance.

"Do you ever miss it?" he said, his words cutting through the quiet like the edge of a serrated blade.

"Miss what?" I asked.

"The sun. Waking up on a brisk fall morning, its rays piercing through the early fog, casting a golden haze over the earth. I miss that."

Sage looked to him with longing sadness.

"I could hardly tell you what it's like," I said. "I don't remember my mortal life. I remember the sun, I know what it is, but I have no memory of ever seeing it. Ever watching a sunrise or sunset."

He turned to me from his chair, as if to convey to me the small pity he felt. Sage picked at a loose string on her jacket. Ralph turned back and gazed down at the floor as if the rotting boards were a marvelous display of art, their swirling patterns yearning to be studied.

I was left to my own thoughts. The silence had become less of a comfort and more of a burden; taunting me, torturing me. Did other Awakened feel like I felt? Unable to remember what it was like to actually feel, to know what life was like? Was it better this way—to not be tortured by constant reminders of what your exis-tence can never be again? Or was this, my unfeeling, the real curse? To wander without aim or purpose, just trying to amuse oneself for a potential eternity, seemed a terrible depression. But it was a depression that someone like me—who knew nothing else—could never really know or understand. I could never really know the true horror of this existence. Or the blessing of it. I can know only what I feel. Which is little. Or too much. It's hard to tell sometimes.

When I returned home that night, a black Escalade sat on the road outside my shed and I walked right past it. I was struck with some alien existentialist ennui and I could not care less about the ring or the Regency or the Primus or the Escalade or the blood or my own unlife. Behind me I heard a click and the soft thud of the car door shutting.

"Maaria."

It was the voice of Gabriel. I kept walking.

"Maaria."

I opened the door to my shed.

It slammed shut in my face. Gabriel stood beside me. He moved so quick I hadn't heard him. I looked at him, my shoulders drooping with excess. He wore the same clothes, but now with a thread wrapped around his neck with a talon hanging from it. His jade eyes bore into mine. Trust. My mind was still home to this languor, but it was now also filled with trust. For Gabriel. In that instant I loved him, and I didn't know why. Just knew I always had, since the first time I saw him.

"Maaria," he spoke. Softly, like a feather caressing my ear. "You have been summoned to the bank again. Serafino requests your presence. I will be here two hours after sundown. Make sure you are well fed."

I stared at him in silence and my eyes filmed over with death. I wanted to feel, to remember, to be human, alive. And even his seducing eyes and the siren song of his voice hadn't been able to stir me.

"Okay," I said. My voice flat.

And then something like compassion made his eyes soften. His hand grazed my face; he caressed my hair. It was like love. And then he leaned in and kissed me on the forehead. The coldness of my skin succumbed to his perfectly soft and perfectly full lips, to their odd warmth. And I swear I heard him whisper gently in my ear, "I'm so sorry."

And then his touch was gone. And he was gone. And then the Escalade was gone. And I was alone. And I walked inside my shed and I fully welcomed the torpid sleep of the morning.

Chapter Fourteen

J UST AS GABRIEL INSTRUCTED ME TO DO, I went out and fed, and the warm vitality of life brought back to me some of the vigor that had been drained from me the night before. I went to some squalid little bar and a girl kept staring at me. As annoying as it was and as tempting as it was to feed from her, it was much easier to just flirt with a drunk and sleazy man for a few minutes, promise to take him back to your place, and then take him around the corner and suck on his neck.

The Escalade pulled up and out stepped Gabriel. I felt that same surge of romance at the sight of him. He, however, did not display any of the warmth he had last night. He opened the door and closed it behind me. Some indie band rolled out of the speakers as he drove us to the bank—the only sound for the whole drive.

When we pulled into the parking lot of the West Gate Bank, the routine was the same as the first time. Open the door for me. Take out keys. Unlock the door. Lead me to the elevator. Go to the last door on the right. Knock. The eyeless butler welcomes me inside. Gabriel leaves. The door closes. I am offered a goblet of blood. The butler leaves. I wait.

The door in the back of the room creaked open and it was only Serafino and the vampire named Dario who walked in. He closed the door behind them. Something about Dario's aloof and lifeless face, with those mis-matched eyes was so unsettling. It was emotionless horror. Serafino led the way, walking toward me. They sat down in the two chairs opposite me, coffee table furnished with my untouched goblet between us.

Broadening his shoulders and folding his hands in front of him, Serafino spoke. "Welcome back and thank you for coming, Maaria. I do have a request to make of you, but first, I believe it is time we receive an update from you. Have you uncovered any information about the Ring of Solomon that may be of use to us?"

A strange rush of confidence surged through me and I jeered, "Hasn't your Primus remembered anything?"

His blood red eyes boiled with anger for half a moment and I caught the tiniest smirk curl up the corners of Dario's lips.

"The Primus," Serafino said, "is not of any concern to you. What you should be concerned about is the consequences you will suffer should you not fulfill your duties here with my Regency. We do not take this partnership lightly. Now," he licked his lips "have you learned anything about the ring?"

Did they not know anything of what we had discovered? Clearly that meant they weren't watching my every move. They didn't know anything.

I answered carefully, trying to control the tremor of lies in my voice. "I've learned more about the ring, but I don't know where it is, where it could be. I know Solomon controlled demons and other preternatural creatures with it. He could talk to animals and control the elements." I paused. "And I know the ring was thrown in the ocean and swallowed by a fish, where it disappeared forever."

Serafino grinned. "Well, that clearly isn't true now, is it Maaria?"

"How should I know?"

He crossed his legs, the sardonic grin on his face becoming a grimace. He seemed to be straining to maintain his disciplinary restraint. Dario, on the other hand, seemed amused. The corner of his mouth trembled and there was—for the first time—a tiny glimmer of life in his eyes.

"What can you tell me about the mutilated gravesite of one Reverend Barth? Dug up not once, but twice. What can you tell me about that, Maaria?"

I stammered, "I…I don't—"

"I do read the newspaper, Maaria. I know what happened."

"It was empty," I said. "I don't…I don't know who the guy is—"

"A vampire," he said. "But our first order of business with you is not Barth, but your little friend, who does nothing but cause trouble. Aasurakasa."

I shook my head and my eyebrows scrunched together in confusion.

"I believe," Serafino continued, "she calls herself Annabelle."

"Oh."

"She is dangerous to us. She threatens our motives. And we cannot afford for her to exist any longer. I—"

"No. No no no no," I interrupted. "I can't."

Dario was getting more and more amused by the minute. A full-out grin threatened to break out on his face.

"Yes," said Serafino. "You will. You will kill her, or I will kill you. There is no negotiation here. Surely, you remember the promise you made the last time you were here, Maaria. I will, of course, offer you anything you need to get the job done. I trust you have a stake?"

I nodded and pulled it out of my pocket. His eyes followed and an ugly frown disfigured his face.

"Dario," he said, nodding his head once.

The slightest twitch of his eyes at his name. He stood up and went to the back of the room, bringing back a small duffle bag. He plopped it on the coffee table and the blood in the goblet splashed up; a single drop landing on the table.

"Are you not thirsty?" said Serafino.

I didn't reply. Dario unzipped the bag. He pulled out a gun and a small glass bottle with a cork stopper in it.

"You will take this gun with you," Serafino said, looking into the chamber, "it is loaded with incendiary rounds—enough to kill her, even if you miss once or twice. And this little vase. Bottle some of her ashes after you have killed her. I will not settle for anything less, I will not settle for simply your word that she is gone."

I took the gun and the bottle and pocketed them. I didn't like this at all. Slowly, and I'm sure with a look of disgust on my face, I walked from the room.

"Good luck," a voice said with a British accent.

I turned back. It was the first time I had ever heard Dario speak. Before I left, Serafino stood, walked over to me, and shook my hand. Those red eyes drove into me and his cold touch sent my skin crawling.

THE ELEVATOR DOORS OPENED TO THE ground floor and Gabriel stood there waiting. Once we were inside the Escalade, he asked, "Where to, Maaria?"

I sighed. "Give me a minute." And he started driving. I pulled out my phone and texted Annabelle. Or Aasurakasa, apparently.

I learned something you need to know about. Meet me in the woods across from the church.

Minutes later she responded.

"Take me to the church," I told Gabriel.

He pulled over to the side of the road about a mile from the church and I walked the rest of the way there. Once I got close, I stopped, pulled the gun out, closed my eyes. Feeling the strange power in my blood, feeling it stir and tremble, I opened my eyes and the gun in my hands was invisible. Up ahead, I saw the black fog looming behind the church. Of course she wouldn't wait where I had asked of her. I crossed the road, silently as possible, and saw the glow of her yellow eyes peer through the blackness and fix themselves on me.

When I was close enough, I did the only thing I could. I aimed the gun at her and fired.

Boom.

It hit. Fire cracked through her veins, like bolts of lightning and molten lava. She looked up at me in utter shock. I shot again. This time, a gaping hole formed in her stomach, oozing with burning blood. She stumbled back. I charged at her. Took the stake from my pocket. She turned, tried to run. I tackled her. Her legs were flying all over, her elbows in my face. I forced her over onto her back, still trapped under my weight. Took my stake out and raised it above my head. Thrust down. A guttural yell sounded and then the stake met her heart.

Silence.

She fell limp.

Motionless.

Eyelids half shut, the yellow beneath them dim and lusterless.

I was panting. Fear. Then adrenaline.

I shoved myself off her. How could this be so easy? It didn't matter. I aimed the gun at her already lifeless body and fired. One. Two. Three. Four. With each shot, the oozing lava poured from her veins more and more intensely, brighter and brighter. And then it engulfed her. Slowly, it hardened—burnt, cracked flesh, blacker than the night sky.

And it crumbled to ash. Dust.

I was gasping. My chest heaving. I let out a terrified laugh. It sounded strange in my ears, foreign, like it hadn't really been me who made the sound. I bent down. Scooped some of her ashes into the bottle and shoved the stopper back in place. And I ran. I didn't look back. I didn't think about what had just happened. I couldn't comprehend it. She was gone. And it was that easy. I killed her. Her final death. There was no second chance for her.

I don't remember much of the ride back to the bank, I only know I was shaking. And then Gabriel led me up to the room again, but this time it wasn't the eyeless butler who opened the door, it was Dario. All previous amusement was gone from his face—just blank and emotionless again. Serafino sat in the same chair as he had when I left, his legs still crossed in the same manner.

I walked past Dario and crossed the room slowly, jaggedly; I was still recovering from the shock. The bottle dangled from my hand, held limply between my thumb and forefinger. I tossed it to him. He caught it and his thin lips broadened into a sick grin. It was venomous the way his fangs jut out; the grin itself was twisted, demented, grotesque. He was a monstrosity of godlike proportions.

I backed away, disgusted and frightened. Then hands placed themselves firmly on my shoulders. I spun my head around and Dario was dragging me to the red velvet chair I sat on before I left. He pushed me down until I sat and he held me there. Serafino got up from his seat and picked up the untouched goblet from the table. A demented grin distorted his face as he neared me and tipped the goblet, letting the blood pour into my mouth.

A moment of blackness.

"Well done," Serafino said. The two of them stood in front of me now, the goblet of blood back on the table still quite full.

I felt the tremors start up in my hands again. I stumbled up and backed away, feet carrying me quicker than when I first tried to leave. I didn't bother to shut the door behind me, just kept backing away. Dario's face was the last thing I saw before he gently shut the door. My eyes may have deceived me, but I swear I saw a wink. Click. The door shut. Click. It was locked.

I bumped into something solid behind me. I started, but breathed a sigh of relief when it was only Gabriel. He led me downstairs and drove me back to my shed. Not a word was spoken. Not a glance was shared. He stopped the car and I got out before he had time to open the door for me. I rushed inside and lay on my bed. My head was a whirling dervish of fears and questions. The walls spinning all around me.

Was I really that upset about killing her? Did it really bother me that much? No, it didn't. I couldn't care less about the bitch. It was just the suddenness of it. I was thrown into it without any choice. It was the ease of it—how quickly and without warning her life could disappear. She had no idea she was going to die. I didn't even give her time to come to terms with it. Didn't even give her time to speak, to say one single word. It was just over, done, gone forever. That is what got to me.

I reached into my pocket for the gun from Serafino. I didn't have any ammo left, but it was still another gun. The touch of cold metal felt oddly calming. I pulled it out.

But it wasn't a gun. It was my stake. It didn't make any sense. I tried to rationalize, but there was no way. The gun, sure Serafino could have slipped it from me. After all, I did black out for a second. But how did I have my stake? I know it was my stake. They didn't replace it. This was mine. I knew it so well now; there was no mistaking it.

But it shouldn't have been my stake. I never picked it up. I ran. I ran and I left it behind in that miserable pile of ash.

Chapter Fifteen

I DIDN'T WANT TO LEAVE MY SHED WHEN I woke. It felt dangerous and the walls surrounding me and closing me in felt so comfortable and safe. I didn't want to face the Regency again, though I felt it was inevitable. I didn't want to think about how they had taken the gun from me. I didn't want to think about how my stake was in my pocket instead. I didn't want to think about the fact that I felt not even a hint of remorse for killing Annabelle. Aasurakasa. Whatever the hell her name was. And I didn't want to cross the place where she had smoldered to ash. I didn't want to think about Gabriel or Sage or Ralph or anyone. I didn't want to think about the ring or our next move toward finding it. I didn't want to face reality.

I walked outside and the wind howled and turned into screams. Everywhere I turned, the shadows of branches seemed to twist and contort themselves in the same way Annabelle's looming black fog did. The shrieks of the wind sounded like her cursing me. And when I stepped from the trees, I found myself on the edge of campus. A rotting white gazebo before me. There should be writhing shadows there. But there weren't. It was empty as I was, desolate as I felt, and rotting as my body should be.

I jumped over the railing, sat down and leaned myself against it. A girl sauntered through the maze of cars, headed toward me. A flame flickered and went out, leaving a small orange glow and a waft of smoke. I pulled the hood of my sweatshirt further over my eyes and waited. In front of my foot was a little red stain in the wood—the drop of Annabelle's blood that flew from her hair. Like I needed any more reminders of the fact that I had ruthlessly taken her life from her. The footsteps neared and neared, becoming louder and louder and I anticipated the startled gasp from the girl when she would finally see my hunched over form sitting there.

And there it was. She jumped a little, too.

"Ohmygod! I didn't see you there!"

I didn't respond and could tell she felt uncomfortable. I don't know what prompted me to do it, but suddenly I pretended to cry. At least I told myself it was only an act. But part of me still thinks those were real tears I shed. My shoulders shook, my nose sniffled, I felt the wetness of tears trickling down my face. It was humiliating. But I told myself: *It's just an act, Maaria. It's just an act.*

She knelt down beside me, her awkward discomfort unwavering as ever. I heard the soft whoosh of air being sucked into her lungs as she was about to speak. To comfort me. But I wouldn't let her. In a wink, I turned and took her. Hands gripping her arms so tight no blood could possibly pass through them; fangs sunk deep into her supple neck. Only a hushed gasp escaped her before she succumbed to the ecstasy. Her heart thumped against me, straining harder as I drank even more.

The sound of tinkling bells littered the air. Someone was calling me. It would have to wait. I sucked harder, her throat eagerly exposing itself, inviting me to take more—which I did. Her lips brushed my ear and she moaned into it. All soft and delicate. I pulled ever harder from that sweet vein and I felt the sudden desire to feed it back to her—her blood, my blood. Just a touch. But I wanted to make her mine, a blood slave. The sadism of it inveigled me.

But then the bells interrupted again, tinkering so innocently in the scene of a murder. I could barely hear it over the resounding thumps of her heart within me, filling me. Hastily, I pulled out my phone. Sage.

I ripped my fangs from the girl's neck. Blood spurted and she slumped to the ground, unconscious.

"What?" I answered. "I'm kind of in the middle—"

"You bitch. You miserable…" The voice rambled on, muffled. But it wasn't Sage. I knew that much. It wasn't her voice. There was no sandpaper grating her words.

"Who is this?" I interrupted.

A cackle erupted, piercing my ears. "Who the fuck do you think this is?"

Beside me, the girl's breathing was getting ragged, shortening.

"What the hell were you thinking going to the Regency? You scum, you…" The voice rambled on.

Short wheezing breaths from the girl. She was dying. I had drunk too much.

"She put you up to this didn't she? I know she did. That pathetic fucking leech. It was her idea, I know it was, don't lie to me."

"I don't understand what the hell you're talking about," I hissed into the phone, struggling to keep my voice down.

"Sage," the voice boomed. "Sage, she fucking betrayed me, us, she—"

"I didn't. Do shit," said a distant voice, strangled somewhere in the background.

The voice growled. "Shut up," it snarled. "And you, you might want to get here, Maaria, before things get a little too…heated."

A whoosh.

A blood-curdling scream.

A childish giggle.

The line went dead.

Full-fledged panic exploded in me. Everything was a blur. I knew the girl was going to die; there was no way around it, but there needed to be a valid reason for it.

My head was spinning and I did the only thing I could think to do. I took the stake from my pocket and plunged it into her neck. Once. Twice. A third time. Fury increasing with every stab. Blood gushed from her neck in spurts and spewed out of her mouth. And I ran. I ran so fast I could have won a goddamned Olympic gold medal.

I knew they were at the cabin. And I knew it was Annabelle on the other end of that call.

I burst through the cabin door with full force. In the middle of the room, strapped to a chair with iron cuffs around her wrists and ankles was Sage. And standing next to her—wicked grin on her face and blowtorch in her hand—was Annabelle.

"It's about time," she said, vowels dancing manically. "Why don't you tell me what's going on, because your little friend here hasn't been so inclined to do so." She gave a villainous smirk.

"I didn't do anything," Sage growled. "I didn't tell her to do anything."

"Don't lie, you filthy whore."

Sage spit at her.

Annabelle's yellow eyes hardened and she wiped the spit from her face. "Tisk tisk," she said, raising the blowtorch. Flames engulfed Sage's face and an agonizing scream bellowed out from them.

"Stop it!" I yelled.

The flames disappeared, leaving Sage's blackened and bubbling flesh heaving in anguish. And she passed out.

"Are you going to tell me what happened, Maaria? I suggest you do or you're going to find yourself in the same boat as her. Why would you go to the Regency?" She cocked her head and her bottom lip jut out in a pout, playing like I had hurt her nonexistent feelings.

I stared at her. "How are you alive," I breathed.

She laughed. "What?"

"How are you even alive?" It came out as a whisper.

Shaking her head, she scoffed, "How delusional are you? I'm alive as I've ever been, maybe more so." She smirked, but it quickly vanished into a cold seriousness. "Now. Why don't you tell me—"

"They would've killed me if I said no. I had to go or they would kill me. They asked me to help them find the ring, offered me rewards. I couldn't say no. If either one of you want me to help you destroy the god forsaken thing, I couldn't say no. Or I wouldn't be here to do it."

She cocked her head in confusion. "They invited you?"

"Yes," I said, "they invited me. She didn't lie, Sage didn't—"

A loud howl brought my words to an abrupt end.

A wolf ran through the door. Ralph. He snarled and snapped his jaws at Annabelle, his fur standing on end.

She glowered at him. "Well, I suppose this is my cue to leave then."

Ralph continued in a low growl, edging closer to her, threatening her.

"Get her out of the cuffs," I said.

She looked at me deadpan, almost rolled her eyes. Her hand dug into her pocket and pulled out a pair of keys. She tossed them behind her, where they clattered against the back wall.

She looked at Ralph. "Go fetch."

His jaws snapped at her once more and she walked past us and out the door. Her black fog engulfed her and she disappeared into the trees.

Ralph immediately shifted into his human form and clambered over to Sage, stroking her hair and brushing over her face, attending to her wounds. I scooped up the keys and brought them over, freeing her one limb at a time.

Chapter Sixteen

THE LAST THING I WANTED TO DO THE following night was meet with Annabelle so she could desperately try to redeem herself, but that is exactly what I did. And I did it out of fear. I didn't want to be the next one bound and burned. I didn't want to find myself on the bad side of someone who could resurrect themselves from the final death, could rise from they ashes like some sort of phoenix. It was the first time I felt genuinely threatened by her, but I have to admit I was also driven by some deep curiosity. So when she asked me to meet her at the gazebo again, I said yes, but we'll have to meet somewhere else. I didn't tell her why, but as I imagined, she didn't care and didn't ask.

When I arrived in the clearing in the woods, she was nestled in the curve of a tree that sprouted almost parallel to the ground before it curved up to the sky.

No black fog loomed around her. I couldn't imagine it being a genuinely courteous gesture. We didn't greet each other. I simply leaned myself against a tree and stared her as she stared back at me.

Finally, Annabelle said, "I'm sorry—"

"Save it. We both know that's not true. Okay? You can explain yourself all you want, justify it all you can, but don't apologize."

Silence.

"Why did you do it, anyway?" I asked. "You didn't need to, you could've just read her mind."

She smirked. "It was more fun this way."

White-hot rage exploded in me and spread across my face.

"What?" she said. "You told me not to apologize."

She pushed herself off the tree and walked over to me, taunting me, and enjoying every second. "Speaking of reading minds…" I could smell the iron on her breath. "I know you're curious as to why Sage has such a strong distaste for me and I know she refuses to talk about it. I could tell you. But only if it will reaffirm our alliance. I don't want you to go backstabbing me afterward or you're going to end up worse off than her. Deal?"

I stared at her with eyes hard as stone, but inside I was dying to know. And yet again, I let my curiosity best me.

"Deal."

She grinned and sat herself on the tree.

"I've been dead for almost ninety years now. And sixty of them have been hell. You call me Annabelle—that was my mortal name—but after I was Awakened, I was given the name Aasurakasa. Dark soul, evil soul, whatever. My Sire's name was Abrigor, the leader of the Tribe of Djall, and one of the group's most powerful leaders in history. I loved him. We were…inseparable. I belonged to him and him to me. This ring I wear—it's his. He coaxed the ritual out of a Shrine member, then killed them and used their very ashes to make the ring. It's all I have left of him.

"We lived in this abandoned hotel. Our whole tribe did. This little town called Maribel, a few hours north of here. And those poor mortals, oh they were the subjects of our reign of terror. But the imbeciles thought we were demons, knights of hell unleashed by black magic." She fought of a fit of her childlike giggles. "Stupid. But then those fools found a real witch—a white witch. And she knew what we were. Started picking us off one by one. She killed Abrigor. *My* Abrigor. The only thing I had. And it was that precious Sage of yours that saved me from the same fate.

"I owed my life to her, Maaria. I was grateful, believe it or not. She saved me, how could I not be?

And we ran down here together. But then she told me to stay away from her, that we weren't companions, that it meant nothing to her, that she wouldn't have saved me if she knew who I was. Can you believe that? Because the Shrine and the Tribe are *so* fucking different. There's only one real difference and I should have been the one to curse her, for worshiping some petty demon—the Almighty Lilitu!—who created us all. The Tribe worships the real creator, the one who created even Lilitu—Father Djall. Father of demons, father of Awakened, Father of all Evil and Darkness. Satan, himself.

"So she told me, 'oh, we'll exist in peace, you don't bother me, I don't bother you. But keep your distance, don't talk to me, don't associate yourself with me in any way.' Scum, she called me. Scum. All because I gave credit where credit was really due." She paused. "That's why she hates me. Because I'm a Tribe member, because I'm *evil*. And her prejudice toward me is why I hate her. But even in the light of a common goal, she refuses to work side by side with a devil worshipper. So she deserved it, all right. After sixty years of bullshit animosity, she had it coming."

Dead quiet as I took it all in.

Without showing the tinge of sympathy I felt, I said, "How do I know you're not lying?"

"Do I have a reason to lie to you?"

"To get me to let it all go and help you with the ring, for starters."

"Make of it what you will," she said, "but don't expect me to act kindly to her. And don't you dare try and go backstabbing me now that you know the truth. Don't forget I'm the one who told you the truth, either. Your sister's still keeping secrets."

"Right," I said. And walked away.

Truth be told, I did pity her a bit. Sage didn't hate Annabelle because of some opposing ideology between the Shrine and the Tribe. Sage didn't believe any of it and she didn't associate herself with anyone. But Annabelle's coven and Sire died, the one who saved her kicked her to the curb, and she lived alone and believing a lie for sixty years. Part of me understood why she was who she was.

WHEN I GOT BACK TO MY SHED, SAGE WAS standing outside holding a plastic bag. Her hair was down, not in its usual braid. It covered her ears and the remaining burns on her face, but most of them had healed in a single night.

"What are you doing here?" I asked.

"Where have you been?"

"Touché..."

She smirked.

"So the ring," I said. "We need to figure out how we're going to find it. We're running out of time."

"No," she said. "One night. One night where we get to forget about all this. It's the best day of the year."

"What's that?" I asked.

"It's Halloween," she smirked. "And we're going out to the bars to have a little fun." She reached into her bag and pulled out two headbands with furry cat ears attached to them. A sly grin crossed my face as she handed one to me. "Besides," she said, "Ralph is staying in to research. I borrowed his lock pick to steal these."

Together we walked into town, with no need to hide, no need to cover our eyes. This was the only time of the year where our feline qualities passed as something mundane. It was liberating.

"You know…" I said, wanting to tell her about my last visit with the Regency, but not knowing if I should. I wanted her to have all the answers for me—why Annabelle was alive, why the gun was gone, how I had my stake instead. But I didn't talk about these things. "Aren't you furious? You seem so calm. For what she did to you, you seem so calm."

"I am furious, Maaria." Her crystal blue eyes drilled into me, and the way her loose curls draped her face in disarray made her look even more wild and fierce than usual. "But I'm going to wait. Let my fury simmer until it's boiling and I can't take it anymore. And when she least expects it, that's when I'll strike. And I'll get my revenge."

I only nodded.

The second we opened the door to the bar, we were welcomed by absolute debauchery. An endless cascade of booze and testosterone, hollering and long legs. Nurses and firemen gyrated; Egyptian goddesses and Catholic priests tipped back endless shot glasses.

Fairies and elves pranced about, killers and princesses in flirtatious pursuit; raucous debates between cartoon characters and superheroes. A pirate, a wizard, a ghost, and a rabbit played dice. An angel and a devil stood side by side. A ninja and a skeleton drunkenly threw darts into the unassuming crowd. A party of cheerleaders and witches held up their vodka shots and toasted in shrill voices. A Wall-Street banker, a reverend, and a University professor— complete with elbow patches on his jacket— enthusiastically greeted a giant bud of marijuana, a Jedi, and a slice of pepperoni pizza.

A vampire walked right past us, slurring on about how he 'vanted to suck our blood.' A zombie limped on behind him. A detective, a pope, a pop star, and a grim reaper sipped on expensive cocktails.

The air was a dizzying mixture of alcohol, sweat, and blood that bombarded the senses. Sickening yet enticing. We went slinking through the crowd, flirting and frightening, picking and choosing our prey as we went. Laughing boisterously with these drunk and unsus-pecting mortals, spilling the shots they offered us straight to the ground, wearing wide grins on our faces the entire time. Mortals slurring their words at us, saying:

'Oh my gawwd, your fangs look so real!'

And: 'Hey girl, lemme get that number.'

And a lot of: 'hjal woien glmdal jdlne plakncei levd.'

All of it was exhilarating. The compliments, the touching, the flush of drunken blood in their cheeks, the fearless interaction with a demon like me. I wanted to feed from them all.

Sage came up behind me and tugged on my sleeve. I turned around, huge beaming grin on my face. Her expression was all grim.

"We need to go," she muttered under her breath.

"What, why?" I asked.

"That de—"

"Wooo!" a girl yelled, bumping into us and spilling half her sugary pink drink on my shoes. She looked familiar and I recognized her as the girl I saw in the dive bar two nights ago, before I went to the West

Gate Bank with Gabriel and went on to kill the still alive-and-well Annabelle.

"That detective," said Sage. "And the pope. They're Venatores."

"They're what?" I was shouting over the din of obnoxious carousal and lechery.

"Hunters," she hissed. "Vampire hunters."

Panic set in immediately. I was about to run. Sage must have known what I was about to do because she grabbed my sleeve and hissed in my ear.

"No! Don't run. We can't attract any more attention. Just," she sighed in frustration, "follow me."

"How do you know?" I asked as we performed our way to the exit.

"The patches on their costumes. It's their insignia, how they identify one another when they're on a hunt, or looking for one."

We continued our act, our mortal facade—feigning drunkenness and mimicking what we had done upon our arrival. And there were the detective and the pope, staring right at me as we slipped through the door. Once we were out of immediate sight, we slipped into our camouflage. Sage, invisible as the crisp midnight breeze, and I, as disguised as a stealthy chameleon.

We made it back safely, but the appearance of hunters—of Venatores—only made our matter of finding the Ring of Solomon more pressing. There was opposition on all sides—the Regency, Annabelle, hunters. The idea of safety was now only an illusion.

Once we reached the outskirts of town we parted ways. When I got to my shed, a black Escalade sat parked on the side of the road again. I walked over toward it, but couldn't see anyone inside.

"Over here," said his voice. Gabriel's voice. He leaned against the door of the shed. "Hello, Maaria," he said as I walked to meet him.

I didn't know what to make of him. Something in those eyes of his told me I could trust him so completely even though I knew, in reality, I shouldn't. But at the same time, I felt some subliminal rapport with him, having nothing to do with those olive green eyes, those aventurine eyes, those deep forest eyes. There was always something new in them.

"You have been summoned again," he said, glancing up toward the sky. "Tomorrow night. I'll be here shortly after moonrise. There is no need to feed beforehand, Serafino will provide you with refreshments."

"Wonderful," I replied.

His eyes softened and became almost compassionate. The slightest evidence of a smile played upon his lips and he raised his hand and brushed the hair away from my eyes.

"Your eyes," he whispered. "They remind me of someone I once met, long ago."

Slender fingers traced themselves along my jaw and fell to his side. He walked away without a word and I heard the door of the Escalade open.

I turned and called out, "Who?"

He looked over to me. "You couldn't know," he said, "he is too old, you are too young."

"Tell me anyway," I said. "I want to know."

A small smile. He stepped inside the vehicle, closed the door. The engine rumbled quietly and the window rolled down.

"I believe his name was Mornor."

And he drove away.

Chapter Seventeen

NOT A SINGLE WORD WAS SPOKEN AS Gabriel drove us to the West Gate Bank. The only sound was the soft tapping of his fingers against the steering wheel.

I was hungry. I was irritable. And as promised, the eyeless butler offered me a goblet full of blood when I entered the room and sat on those velvet cushions. It was still warm.

"Embalmed just for you," he said beaming. Crusted puss coated his red and infected eyelids. Just looking at it made me nearly lose my appetite.

He left, I drank the blood, and minutes later the door opened. Serafino led the way, followed by Dario—the right hand man, Damon—the muscle, and Drusilla—the whore. Damon and Drusilla sat in the chairs opposite me. The whore crossed her legs and chewed on her nails, her eyebrows raised at me. She was a con-descending, narcissistic, and crude creature whom I hated almost more than Serafino, even though I'd never heard her speak a single word.

Dario came and pulled the chair next to me over to the others and sat, giving me occasional glances filled with puzzling undertones, like he was silently pleading with me.

After everyone was seated, Serafino stood beside them, folded his hands in front of him, and broadened his shoulders. He was a man of ritual.

"Good evening, Maaria," he said. "You have passed out first—be it hypothetical—test. I am sure you have a few questions and I invite you to ask them before we proceed."

Drusilla stopped biting her nails and focused all her attention on raising her eyebrows even higher at me while she waited for a response.

"You know what my questions are," I said. "Why don't you just explain it."

He frowned. "I think it would be in your best interest, Maaria, to fix you attitude. But, I will be generous this once and do as you ask. Aasurakasa is alive, she never suffered the final death, you did not kill her. An ability of my race—the Valde—learned only by the most capable Awakened, allows one to manipulate and change other's memories. That is what I did to you that night. That is why the gun I had given you had vanished. It is why you had your stake with you instead. It is why Aasurakasa is still alive. None of it happened. While you thought you were on a mission to destroy her, you were, in reality, sitting in the same chair you are now, held in a trance as I implanted the memory. It was, quite simply, a test to see how far you would go to help us. And you passed.

"While you were entranced, I also took a small drink of your sweet nectar and learned a little something about you. You do this for your Sire, do you not? You believe this is a second chance, this is your purpose, your mission. Well, I am giving you an opportunity to fulfill this purpose of yours.

"Now," he continued, giving me no opportunity to speak, "as I am most certain you are aware, we have searched the St. James church for evidence of the Ring of Solomon. The first time, we lost a member of our Regency, and the second, two ghouls. Most recently, my superior—the Primus—has recollected one of his lost memories from the fog, thus informing us of a potential danger, but also a potential indication of the ring's whereabouts. You need not know the details, but understand that it is now your duty to uncover any information you can about the Ring of Solomon and the St. James church and to report back to us within one week.

"Within one week, you must discover the location of the ring and you must inform us of the location. You will not retrieve the ring yourself. Or you will die. Do you understand?"

I stared back at him. "Yes," I said. "I understand."

And I did understand. I understood quite well. But that didn't mean I was going to listen. I had no idea how I was going to keep them in the dark, keep them away from the ring, but I had to. And if that was impossible, then at the very least, I had to hold them at bay just long enough for us to get the ring and destroy it. Before they would destroy me.

Sure, this life was a second chance for me, but if I would die, then I would die. I would disappear from an existence that isn't even a true existence to begin with. And with my final death, I would enter oblivion and this second chance wouldn't matter at all.

Call it bleak, call it whatever you will, but as mesmerizing as I found the clarity in unlife, I knew the future was likely to hold nothing but bleakness. Boredom. A meaningless attempt to amuse oneself and a horrendous attempt to recapture life without the very thing that makes life what it is—life.

NOT FIVE MINUTES AFTER I RETURNED HOME, I got a call from Sage.

"Hey, have you seen Ralph at all?" Her voice shook.

"No, why?"

"It's just...he—he went out to hunt and he should've been back a while ago. I've tried calling him, but he hasn't picked up at all. I'm just...I'm starting to get worried."

I went over to the cabin, told her it was probably nothing, offered suggestions that did nothing to console her. Perhaps he went into the next town, his phone was dead, he was still hungry. And that's when it flooded in, when everything made sense.

Annabelle.

"Maaria," her voice shook, "what's wrong?"

"Does Annabelle have blood slaves at all, do you know?"

"I wouldn't put it past her, why?"

"There was a girl," I said. "I saw her at a bar before I met with the Regency, the night before Annabelle attacked you. She kept staring at me. I saw her again last night at the bar, and now Ralph is gone."

Realization sunk in and she started to panic. I stepped outside and called Annabelle. She picked up.

"Where is he?" I asked.

Giggle. "I don't know what you're talking about, Maaria."

"Do you think they're not going to come after you next?" I said.

"Oh, they'll go after every vampire I tell them about, and, yes, then they'll come after me. But I'll take care of them before they can get that far."

"So where is he?"

"They're Venatores," she said. "They're poor trash, try checking cheap motels. Maybe I'll get lucky and they'll take care of all three of you."

She hung up.

WITH ONLY FOUR MOTELS IN TOWN, IT DIDN'T take long to track them down. We took our cat head-bands with us so we could ask the front desk about the Venatores. To them, it just looked like we were celebrating Halloween a day late. When we finally found them, the door was unlocked and we barged inside. Ralph was bound to a chair. As soon as he saw us, his eyes widened in panic and he shook his head.

"No," he said in a low voice. "No, get out. Leave, Sage. Leave."

Footsteps coming from the bathroom. Footsteps from behind us. An arm wrapped around Sage's neck, knife pointed at her chest. I lurched forward toward Ralph.

"No!" he yelled. "Maaria, don't!"

The hunter lunged at him, and before I could reach him he was staked in the chest. His head fell forward, limp. Behind me, Sage and the other hunter grappled for the knife. I took out my gun.

The man in front of me chuckled. "Oh, you think that's a good idea, do you? Firing off a gun in a motel full of people. Huh? Maaria, is it?"

The pistol shook. He was right. I took out my stake and he took out his own blade and sped toward me. We were a blur of limbs and behind us was another blur of limbs. Sage's voice became all Mornor and sandpaper when she grunted in pain. I caught a glimpse of her. Blood poured from her arm and they became a crimson blur. Ralph still sat motionless in the chair; chin drooping, resting on the stake protruding from his chest.

I was on the floor now, hitting and clawing with this Venatore, when I felt the give of his flesh as my stake sank into his leg. He pushed me off him and I yanked the stake out. I looked back at Sage who had gotten hold of her machete. The lamplight glinted off it as she swung, just missing the man as the edge grazed against his shirt.

I turned back. The man on the ground limped toward a duffel bag of weapons. I lunged at him and he threw his knife at me. I dodged it and slammed the stake into his other leg. Tore it out again. Grabbed the duffel bag and threw it to the back of the room. Turned around again.

The man's hand was wrapped around Sage's arm. He kneed her in the stomach and her machete clattered to the ground. With reflexes nearly as quick as a vampire, he grabbed it, swung at her, and she bent back to avoid it. I charged at him, but the man on the ground behind me grabbed my ankle and I tumbled to the ground.

Sage screamed. A thump. A second thump.

When I looked up, Sage was on her knees.

"N—," she choked back a sob.

I didn't want to look behind me. But I did. And Ralph was no longer there. Just a pile of ash.

"Get up, Sage!" I yelled and climbed to my feet. I jumped on the hunter who killed him; the machete flew from his grasp and I heaved my stake into his side. Blood gushed out. His eyes rolled into the back of his head and he fell unconscious. I looked back and Sage was nowhere to be found. I started toward the other hunter, still limping toward me. He had another knife in his hand, swung it at me, but he was too slow.

I drove my stake into his stomach and he fell to his knees.

A glint of light flashed in the corner of my eye and I swung around to strike. But it wasn't the other hunter. It was a levitating machete. It floated in front of the Venatore with a stake still in his stomach and tilted, letting the light shimmer off the cold, menacing blade.

"No, no please!" he begged, shaking his head, bloody mess of hair matted to the sides of his face.

And she swung. The third thump of the night as he was decapitated and his head fell to the floor, still wearing the ugly expression of his plea. A fourth thump as the rest of his body followed. An echo of Ralph's death—thump, his head fell; thump, his body fell; poof, he's gone. The blade floated toward the other hunter, still unconscious, and seconds later—the fifth and final thump as he met the same fate.

Then the blade vanished and Sage never reappeared. So I did the same; left the scene behind in a state of shock, remorse, and horror.

Chapter Eighteen

I GRIEVED FOR HIM. FOR RALPH. BUT MY grief was in no way comparable to what Sage must have felt. Her own brother, whom she had been miraculously reunited with by an act of God. And after so many years apart. But now he was gone again. And this time it would be forever. Sage would need time to heal, recover from the loss of her brother. But that was exactly what we didn't have. Time. Between the Regency and Annabelle and wanting so desperately to get myself out of this deplorable mess, we didn't have the time to grieve. We needed it, but we did not have it.

As I opened the door to go feed, there was a flutter of something falling to the ground. Wedged between the door and the frame, there fell a piece of parchment. I didn't have the slightest clue how it got there, but I picked it up and read it.

Time is running out
and I am here to help.
Looking in plain sight,
and find me, you just might.
A reverend I once was,
a disciple I still am.
I worship not Lord Jesus,
but instead a different man.
You have searched in my old Synagogue—
you'll find me in another.
A place where blood's been drunk before,
a place to rediscover.
But be careful; watch your step,
it is my duty to guard and to protect.
So if you wish to find the Ring,
just come with good intent.

Forget feeding. I walked right back inside. It didn't matter who had written it, what it meant, or where it would take me. Mention of the Ring of Solomon was enough for me to follow it anywhere.

It must be written by the same man who left the code in the old book at the church. They're both penned on parchment and both a riddle of sorts. Maybe I'd find this person at St. Catherine's. But I hadn't fed there before. Where was somewhere I'd fed before, that I had to rediscover?

The campus. It's a Christian school, so there must be a church or chapel there somewhere—a synagogue.

I'd fed there, but had never come across a chapel. That must be it.

I walked out my door for a second time and bypassed the hunt for blood. We simply didn't have time. To grieve, to feed, nothing.

The ring came before anything.

But the thought of grief sent me to the cabin. The ring would come second on the agenda for just one night.

Sage opened the door with a harrowing look in her eyes. Her grief was understandable, but her inability to deal with Ralph's death was not what we needed right now. She needed time, but we didn't have it and she needed to sacrifice it for one week. Just a single week.

"I picked up a newspaper," she said. Her voice was flat and dead, lacking all evidence of her fiery spunk. "The horrific murders that occurred at a local motel made the front page. Investigators say it's being tied to an auburn-haired man who disappeared from the crime scene. No witnesses. At least we won't be tied to it. No one will come looking for us. They'll just keep looking for an innocent killer they'll never find."

Her blue eyes looked at me, but they seemed almost grey with all her lackluster depression. I wanted to sympathize, I really did, but instead, I slapped her. The loud smack of skin against skin was a stark contrast to the silence around us, the depressing atmosphere. Her face hardened, but she didn't fight back.

"Get your shit together, Sage," I said. "Because if you don't get it together right now, we're going to be in trouble and the Regency will win. And all of this will be for naught. All this pain and suffering and death, for nothing. You'll have all the time in the world to grieve for Ralph after all this is over. After we find the ring and destroy it."

A long silence followed. And finally:

"After we find Annabelle and destroy her. After I get my revenge," Sage said. "This doesn't end until that happens."

"The honor is all yours."

She nodded. Closed her eyes and drew a long breath in and slowly exhaled. "Okay," she said. "You're right. I can do it. I'll help get this done."

"You damn well better," I said. "You said so yourself that I couldn't do this alone. Stay here tonight. I have a lead I have to go look into. But tomorrow, you're helping me. I need you."

I camouflaged myself when I got near campus and followed behind a student to get inside. I wandered and wandered and on the second floor, I came across a sign that pointed the way to a chapel.

I pulled open one of the heavy wooden doors. It was dark inside, but the shiny wooden floors reflected a myriad of colors from the stained glass windows. An organ with over one hundred pipes, some over twenty feet tall sat next to me. In front of me was a small pillar, waist-high, with a bowl of holy water in it. I dipped my finger into it. It was cool; it didn't hiss or sizzle, didn't burn me. Turns out we aren't part demon after all.

A man sat in the front pew. He didn't turn to look who had entered, just continued staring straight ahead. With slow steps I walked down the aisle, like a bride going to meet her husband, and blues, red and yellows decorated my skin. Halfway down the aisle, the man became nothing but a dark silhouette as the soft, warm light glowing from behind the giant crucifix behind the altar swallowed him whole. I watched as a pale pink-white aura glowed around him and let it fade away as I drew closer. When I nearly reached the chancel, lined by the green marble communion rail, I turned to face the stranger.

He sat with one leg resting on the knee of the other. A tall, slender man in suit and tie. He had a small square face with a thick, caterpillar of a moustache resting over his lip. He watched me with a bored look.

"Who are you?" I whispered.

He smiled. "You know who I am."

I was puzzled for only a moment before revelations flooded in, things I couldn't know how I missed. But then I knew. Everything made sense.

"R.G.C.B" I said, a soft incredulity in my voice.

He just smiled back.

My knees felt weak. There was a power emanating from him which, in and of itself, was intimidating, but something about his presence said he wasn't the least bit threatening.

"Reverend G. Christian Barth, pleasure to meet you" he said and patted the pew cushion. "Have a seat."

I was hesitant, but sat myself beside him, leaving a few feet of space between us.

"I want to tell you a bit about myself, Maaria. I want to explain to you who I am. And I want you to understand what is happening here." He talked with his hands as he spoke, but not erratically, it didn't distract you from what he said. Rather, it enhanced it; just gentle, sweeping motions that added grace and meaning to his every word.

"You brought the Ring of Solomon."

"Yes," he said. "But that is only one small part of my story. There is—"

"Are you—I'm sorry. Are you sure it's safe here?"

"I wouldn't bring you here if it wasn't," he said with a thin smile. "May I continue?"

"Yes, of course. I'm sorry," I said.

"Don't be sorry," he said. "Never be sorry. Now, as you may know, I belong to a lineage of Awakened, whom over the ages have protected the Ring of Solomon. It is true the ring was stolen from Solomon by one of his illegitimate sons—a son who had willingly invited the condition of unlife as a means of revenge on his father. It is not true, however, that this is some incredibly long lineage; I am merely the sixth generation. My Sire was called Cormac, before him was Everard, then Damaris, then Nikodemos, and then Nabad himself.

"But Nabad quickly became known as Asmodeus, the demon who threw Solomon's ring into the sea, where it was swallowed by a fish. This was a lie fashioned by King Solomon. He called his son a demon, for in a way, he was. And he told the people it was lost in the sea forever, for he was too proud to admit he had been tricked, defeated.

"Since Nabad, it has been the duty of our lineage, our bloodline, to guard and to protect the ring. It is a noble cause, but it is one I have grown tired of. Maybe one day I will tell you how old I am, but for tonight, just know I am older than most Awakened alive today could ever fathom."

He paused. Stroked his moustache. He looked nearly mortal, though his face had that supernatural quality—pale, firm, his youth preserved through what I imagined were centuries. But despite the ageless skin, his eyes revealed the true weariness he spoke of. I found a hint of sadness in them, but mostly, the spark of life preserved in his body was gone from his eyes. Almost dead. Almost like Dario's.

"Unfortunately," he continued, "however much I may want the ring destroyed, freeing me of my duties, letting me shrug off this burden, I cannot destroy it myself. It is up to someone else. I cannot even give you the location. This duty was passed onto me through the blood; one would think its power is diluted with each generation, but I almost believe the opposite is true. I could not tell you if I tried. You must find it yourself. Which is why I have left these subtle hints. You have deciphered the message I left in the book?"

"Yes," I said, my voice filled with absolute wonder. And it all made sense. A tomb—the sea, a ring—Solomon's ring, a child—a fledgling vampire. I forged man's anthems; and he had, Barth and those before him were responsible for all the tales and myths of King Solomon and his magick ring. The three of us had been right in our guesses.

"And what did you find in it?" he asked.

"Michigan's rolling tides."

The smallest of smiles. "Good. Remember that. Search every nook and cranny if you must. You will find it."

"What about the Regency?" I asked. "The Primus?"

"All I can do is pray you beat them to it. Take whatever help you can and accept the consequences later."

"And what happens if they do beat me to it?"

"Then I will interfere and lay them to rest. And I will take the ring with me and I will disappear with it once more."

Wordless conversation passed silently between us. And then he said, "Now go, free me from this curse."

AS I WALKED FROM CAMPUS, MY INSTINCT was to search the bluff overlooking the lake for any sign of a ring. My instinct told me to do this, but my intuition told me not to. Not tonight, not yet, it said. Barth said our meeting was safe, but what if someone was watching me now? The Regency didn't seem to be keeping an eye on me, but Annabelle's little blood slave could be sneaking about. Walking out of the school to embark on a rampant search would seem suspicious, so I just left and hoped if anyone were spying on me, they'd think I had only fed there.

I didn't know what to make of Barth. He could have stopped this all along. He could have eliminated the members of the Regency, the Prince, taken the ring away. Sage never would have been torched by Annabelle; Ralph never would have needed to die. It was selfish. Selfish to let others suffer and die for something they didn't ask to be a part of. Selfish to watch from the sidelines as they fight in ignorance just because you want the ring destroyed, just because you want to be freed from your duties, just because you don't want to move it away and save us all this pain.

I had been thrown into this unlife without my permission. I had been dragged into this business of the ring without my permission. I had the wishes of the Regency thrusted onto me without being given any alternative. I had lost a friend; Sage had lost a brother. Is this what this existence is? It isn't fair. I didn't ask for this. I didn't want it.

And I would do precisely the same thing as Barth.

That's why he did what he did. He didn't ask for his eternal existence to be consumed by the duty of protecting a ring. He didn't want to anymore. And he was old, I knew that. Centuries old at the very least. And I was only in my first month of unlife. It's no wonder he was willing to let others die to free him from his cause. His curse, he called it. I couldn't imagine what it would be like. The pain of it. I couldn't even imagine living for centuries if I were the happiest vampire in existence. But to live so long in agony...

My phone rang. I didn't recognize the number and was apprehensive about answering. But I choked it back and pressed *Talk*.

"Maaria?"

I aborted all efforts to choke it back. Instead, it intensified and bifurcated into rising alarm and sinking dread. I swung around in a rushed panic and scanned my surroundings.

"What are you... Why are—"

"I don't have much time Maaria," said the thick British accent, "so let me explain myself."

Thoughts teetered back and forth. Hang up or listen, hang up or listen. I listened.

"I despise Serafino just as much as you—if not more. He holds power he doesn't deserve; his sense of superiority is infuriating. I will help you, Maaria. I will help you find the ring. I will help you destroy it without speaking a word to the members of the Regency—or anyone else for that matter—so long as you give me your word that you will help me destroy Serafino after it is over."

Stunned silence.

"How do I know I can trust you?" I asked.

"Because I have nothing left to lose. I have lost my free will, my sense of self-worth. I gave up everything I had to come here, to this great land of promise and opportunity you call America, and I have gotten nothing. I gave everything for nothing in return. And I have Serafino alone to thank for it. That is why you can trust me."

Barth's words flashed back to me—*Take whatever help you can get and accept the consequences later.*

"You have yourself a deal."

"Good." I heard the smile of relief in his voice.

And with that, he hung up.

Chapter Nineteen

T HE WORLD GAVE ME NO TIME TO come to terms with the unexpected turn of events of the night before. I would have to keep moving, keep pushing toward the end game. When I woke, I set out to feed before I would go and search for the ring. I hadn't heard from Sage yet, but I thought it best she contact me first, whenever she felt ready. If I met with her now or in a few hours didn't make much difference. I had been hard enough on her, forcing her to put her grieving aside.

I roamed through the woods, searching for some lonesome creature to fall prey to me and my fangs, but I found nothing, saw nothing, heard nothing. Strange. I walked even deeper into the forest, where the trees encroached upon me and everything became more feral and untamed. But still…nothing.

And then I felt a presence. Some sort of breathe pulsing through the air, the lifeblood of the earth rising up through the dirt, a great élan permeating every atom with a burning heat. It held far too much gravity to be any creature native to the trees. If I had been religious at all, I would have assumed it to be God or an angel. And as I carried on, the energy continued to amplify and swell.

There was a whisper in my ear that spoke my name. I turned around, but there was no one there for as far as I could see. Fear was prodding at me, tapping me on the shoulder. When I turned back around, not twenty feet in front of me, stood a woman in a short white dress, yellowed with age.

She looked mortal, save for the luminous white hair that cascaded down just past her shoulders. It looked almost clear, like a polar bear's fur, but it glimmered like phosphorescent diamonds. Her skin showed no evidence of sick deathly pallor, but was smooth and white as marble, every curve of her body sculpted in absolute perfection. Eyes shimmered with brilliance, the shattered moonlight reflecting hints of violet and azure. She had to be a vampire. Right? But I couldn't know for sure—even her aura showed only a silvery haze.

"You'll find it," she spoke, "in a stone box. A hidden cavity in the stone of the bluff, marked the by the sigil of the Archangel Michael. A spell has been placed on it, and can only be opened by the Holy Lance, the Spear of Destiny, the one which belonged to Longinus."

I was frozen and sputtered out, "How…"

"The Englishman can help you."

"…How do you know?"

But there was only a flutter of air as she disappeared.

Her voice had rung out like a silver bell—crystalline, pure, and somewhat disembodied. It was angelic, it was commanding.

I couldn't fathom how she knew what she claimed, but by now I knew better than to expect a simple answer from anyone. Somehow, though—I knew. I knew she was telling the truth.

But instead of going straight to the campus and searching the bluff, I started in the opposite direction. To Sage's cabin.

THE SECOND SHE OPENED THE DOOR, I KNEW she had entered the second stage of grief: anger. Her aqua eyes were filled with fire. She wanted revenge. But I didn't give her time to fantasize about vengeance—there were more pressing matters. So I told her. About the girl, about the ring, about Dario and his offer to help. And for the first time since this all began, we felt as if we might have a real chance at winning.

We sauntered back through the trees with an airy bounce in our steps. Hope was renewed to us; this was almost over. It was nearly a dance, Sage almost once again that savage ballerina she had been at the start. But her shoulders still sagged with the excess of hollowness.

It wrenched my motionless heart in two to see it, a gaping hole of heavy emptiness floating in the cavity of my chest. Without Ralph, the only emotion she was capable of feeling was anger. And if not anger, then nothing. Even now, when we should be invigorated with hope, she couldn't really feel it. Only an echo. Those echoes that I knew so well.

We got to the campus and bolted down the concrete stairs of the bluff. We reached the bottom, right along the coastline, and began our search. I went off to the left and she to the right, running along the shore and climbing the rocky cliffs. Neither of us knew what to look for, didn't know what the sigil of the Archangel Michael looked like. It was something Ralph would have known. Or at least been ecstatic to research. I think Sage couldn't help but think about this too, and her sadness deepened—or her anger flared—as we continued to search.

"There's something here," she called.

Fifteen feet up, in the rocky wall, she pointed to a tiny, faint symbol. We climbed up with ease, and on one of the rocks was a near indiscernible symbol that looked sort of like the Greek letter Lambda, which I recognized from Barth's code. But instead of being curved, it was formed by sharp angles and a little circle at the end of the line on the left.

It had to be what we were looking for. Why else would such a strange symbol be here? It was a Christian campus, sure, but if it wasn't a cross or some other symbol of Jesus, most would assume it was pagan or a satanic cult. Maybe that was the point of hiding it like this. Who knows, I could be wrong. Only one thing was certain:

This was it.

Sage slammed her fists into the rock and a large chunk loosened. This was really it. I pulled the rock out and inside the cavity was a limestone container the size of a shoebox.

Sage looked at me with wide eyes. "We're gonna fucking win," she said.

I nodded. "We're gonna fucking win."

We shoved the stone back into place and it looked as if we were never there.

As we were walking back, Sage looked to me. "I'm going to kill her, you know."

"I know."

"She stole my brother from me. And all because she thought I told you to go to the Regency. Because she thought I was going to beat her to the ring."

"I'm sorry," I said. And I truly was. "I should have told her I'd been there. This never would have had to happen. Ralph would still—"

"Shut up," she said. "You shut the hell up, Maaria. This isn't your fault." She looked down at her feet, "If anything, it's mine. I saved her life, you know. And now she hates me because I didn't…I don't know. I didn't give her an opportunity to save mine. I pushed her and her macabre beliefs away and this is what I get."

This was her first mention of her past with Annabelle and I realized how much they completely misunderstood each other. Of course, I didn't mention to Sage that I knew any of this. It wasn't the time. It would never be the time. She would tell me her story when she saw fit, and I would pretend it was the first time I'd heard it.

"But I'll kill her," she continued. "I swear to god, I will rip her limb from limb and I will watch her burn. She'll beg for death after I'm through with her."

She was silent for a long moment.

"And then I will send her to hell."

WHEN SAGE AND I PARTED FOR THE NIGHT, I sent out a message to Dario.

We need to talk. Where can we meet?

And then I waited. Half an hour later, my phone rang.

"Maaria?" he said.

"Yes."

"We have to be careful. Gabriel will pick you up. He will blindfold you. But he will take you to me. It is a safe location, but we won't have a lot of time, you understand."

"Okay," I said. "When can I—"

"He'll be there at half–twelve."

Click.

At precisely twelve thirty, the familiar Escalade pulled up to my shed. Gabriel stepped out and opened the back door for me. As I walked, those green eyes stared at me as they always did and I felt I could trust him—as I always did. But it was different somehow. That intense beam of trust seemed to have gone away, melted into something more human, like the way a husband looks at his bride.

He blindfolded me as instructed and closed the door behind me. I think it was then—while I was left with nothing but my thoughts—that I really realized how differently things were turning out from what I had expected. I came into this thinking I needed to rid myself of humanity. And I tried so hard to do it. At first, I couldn't feel anything, save for fear, excitement, and apathy; the rest were just those faint echoes of emotions I once knew. But now. Now I was feeling despair and sympathy and friendship and anguish and guilt and tranquility and compassion and this strange thing like love.

I was more human than ever before.

The car slowed and started twisting around in every direction. When we finally came to a stop, Gabriel came around back and peeled the cloth away from my eyes, letting me out of the vehicle. I stepped onto gravel. Benches and trash bins were scattered around us. A park.

"Follow the trail to the left," he whispered and rest a hand on my shoulder. "You'll find him there."

I looked at him with curiosity and asked, "Do you know why we're here? Really?"

He smiled. "It's my job to do what I'm told by my superiors. Not to ask questions."

He turned and got back in the front seat, closed the door and turned off the lights. I set off on the trail with gravel crunching lightly under my feet. Around the second curve, I saw him. His haunting mismatched eyes stared at me in the same austere way they always did.

"I know where it is," I said.

His eyes widened with a childlike innocence, like a kid who'd just been told he could eat candy for dinner. But there was no glimmer of greed or excitement. Just simple surprise. And I believed I could really trust him.

"Where?" he asked.

I hesitated. "You'll need a lance. The Holy Lance."

"The Lance of Longinus?"

"So I'm told...yeah."

His brow furrowed in confusion. He closed his eyes and pinched his nose, giving me a moment's comfort from their unnerving quality. "Alright," he heaved, "we'll have to act fast. The Primus will notice it's missing, but I think I can manage it. Where is it, exactly? The ring?"

"The campus," I said. "Down by the bluff. There's a stone with a sigil on it. Behind it in this little cavity is a stone box. With a spell. It can only be opened by striking it with the lance."

He tilted his head. "Curious. Gabriel will take you back to town. Meet me there tomorrow night, not an hour after moonrise. And be prepared to fight. I'll bring what I can, but you'll need whatever weapons you might have."

I nodded. A fretful storm of anxiety rumbled in my mind as I turned to leave. But my curiosity got the best of me and turned me around. "Why are you doing this?" I asked.

He smirked, a hint of life sparkling in his eyes. "I'm a self-serving man. I never had any real loyalty to Serafino, the Regency, or the Nobilis Sanguis. And frankly, I'm just sick of it."

"And what happens when this is over?"

"We go our separate ways."

I nodded and turned to leave.

"And Maaria," Dario called behind me, "remember your part of the deal."

I stopped and turned back, looking him dead in the eyes for the first time.

"How could I forget?"

Chapter Twenty

M Y EYES BLINKED OPEN. TONIGHT was the night. It might be the last night. I grabbed my gun and my stake and walked outside to wait for Sage. The air was eerily still; the only sound was the lone mournful call of an owl somewhere in the distance.

I heard somewhere once that hearing the hoot of an owl meant someone was going to die.

As I waited, the thirst arrived. With long Nosferatu fingers, it dug itself deep inside my skull. I needed to feed. If this was going to turn into a fight, I was going to need a clear head.

I looked up. The sky was dark; no moon or stars pierced through the thick haze of clouds. They were solid, towering monuments, leaning over me, closing in on me, staring down at me. It felt like a warning.

Don't you dare, young lady. Tonight we bring only death and despotism.

I remember the last words I thought to myself before Sage appeared and I would no longer be able to think, only act:

There will be no tomorrow.

"HAVE YOU FED?"

Sage walked toward me and I shook my head. She tugged the sleeve of her jacket up, revealing the milk white skin of her wrist.

"Here," she said. "Drink."

Déjà vu.

Another owl hooed overhead. Two deaths.

"Are you sure?" I asked her.

"We don't exactly have time to waste do we?" There was edge to her voice; sharp as the blade she always kept hidden beneath her coat.

I knelt down, wrapped my lips tightly around her wrist and drew the blood from her veins to mine. Just like with Mornor. I thought of the owls. Perhaps this was our relationship coming full circle before one or both of us would die. We were made sisters by the same Sire and now we would give to each other like he had given to us. The thought of our deaths was daunting, but as her blood filled me and the clarity came, adrenaline shattered all worries. I gingerly pulled my fangs from her wrist. She twisted her ring, throwing a shadow over us, and we ran like hell.

By now everyone knew. Sage and I, Annabelle, the Regency, the Primus, anyone and everyone knew. The ring was no secret any longer. And this was a race to the end of the world.

The navy black sky swirled chaotically, monuments which towered ever higher. And here we were, all up bright and early—or however one would phrase it—racing to the end of the world, going nowhere.

All the way to the campus entrance, across the lawns and the asphalt, down the flights of concrete stairs, standing on the rocky shore of Lake Michigan's rolling tides, not a word was spoken between us. The only sound was that of the gentle waves and a third owl's call, signaling another imminent destruction.

Sage twisted her ring again, surrendering us to the subtle starlight. We waited in a mutually understood silence, listening to the gentle clapping of waves rolling over the rocky shore.

A soft crunching behind us signaled Dario's arrival. He carried a sack over his shoulder and wore his best suit. In his free hand, he held what I could only assume was the Holy Lance. Sage rested her hand on her hip, ready to draw her machete, as he approached. Dario's expressionless eyes glanced over us like the reality of the coming events didn't trouble him at all.

"Can we trust him?" Sage muttered under her breath.

The sudden sounds of speech were jarring and I only nodded.

Dario dropped his sack to the ground and opened it, pulling out guns. He took them out one by one, checking each of them—all fully loaded and equipped with a silencer. This was important. If it were going to come to gunfire, we'd need to be stealthy as the school was barely one hundred yards from us.

"You'll need these," he said. His accent was heavier than normal. "Incendiary rounds."

I took mine, but Sage refused. "Just take it," I said. "There'll be more of them than there are us."

But she wouldn't budge. Stubborn even to the end of the world. "I have my blade," she said. "I'll be fine."

Her voice was all sandpaper now.

I wanted to push her into taking it, but Dario simply shrugged and chucked it far into the dark waters of the lake. A hushed splash followed by a moment of silence as we watched it get pulled under the tides.

"It's hard to tell if this is an end or a new beginning," I said.

Dario shrugged. "It's a mad world, Maaria. I don't have an answer. No one does. We're all just running in circles." Those divergent eyes looked right through me, deader than they've ever been before. And far above us, far away, I heard a fourth owl call out.

The muffled noise of an engine hummed above us and we drew our weapons. It would come to a fight. Seconds later, the tall broad silhouette of Serafino, head of the Regency, came barreling down the stairs.

This was real. This was really happening.

He was followed by the muscle and the whore— Damon and Drusilla. A neckless fool and a whirlwind of red hair whipping in the wind. Between them walked the eyeless butler. And right behind them: Gabriel. He ran down the bluff, the wind blowing his curls over his eyes. But then he saw me and for that small moment, time stopped. The most apologetic look floated along an invisible wire, from him to me.

And then he looked away, breaking our bond, and continued down the stairs toward our fight.

I fell back into myself; a brief intermission from reality that I wished could last forever. I whipped around and saw all these familiar faces, nearly every face I knew in this unlife, all gathered in this familiar place.

Serafino fired the first shot. And with it, the sky opened up. Black, swirling masses of pandemonium towering ever higher as it parted in two, revealing an empty sky as thunder roared. It was moral anarchy. Mirroring our fate and mocking us—the meaninglessness of a war between dead men walking.

Another gunshot. But bullets only took us so far. Once we were all on an even playing field, all gathered on the jagged, rocky shore, we became a giant blur of fists. Bodies crashing into bodies with resounding thuds, fists connecting to faces, the blur of bodies flying across the shore. The spraying of blood and teeth was eclipsed by the darkness. The senseless violence was obfuscated by the twin tower cover of clouds.

In the periphery, I noticed a writhing fog too black to be rolling in from the lake. Annabelle.

Red lips. Red hair. A fist crashed into my jaw. Merlot blood spewed from my mouth as I was caught in the balance between the opposing forces of the earth and the sky. Yellow eyes. Annabelle. I crashed to the ground. The two of them became a flurry of yellow and red. I pushed myself to my feet to join the fight.

A ton of bricks crashed into me and tackled me to the ground. Damon was on top of me. He was stronger than me, but I fought him as best I could. I finally threw him off me and as I rolled over to get up, a stream of fire flew from a little glass bottle held in Annabelle's hands. Flames danced around Drusilla. A fist sent my chin crashing into teeth. Bone against bone. The fire went out and Annabelle tossed the bottle over her shoulder.

Damon and I threw punch after punch and I caught the glint of a machete fly past me. Knee to stomach. Fist to face. Hand to throat. I heard the clatter of metal falling against the rocks somewhere to the right. The stir of anxiety it brought distracted me and my body flew over Damon as he threw me to the ground. My back cracked against the hard earth.

Yellow eyes. Sage's machete in Annabelle's hand. A body crumbled to ash before her.

I don't know what I screamed at her. Of if I said anything at all. The boiling rage blacked everything out. So many feelings rushed through me, so intense that it felt like nothing at all. I had just watched my companion and sister crumble to ash, the final blow from her own weapon. Suddenly Gabriel was there, pulling me back. My throat was raw and tears stained my face. He was whispering in my ear, but I didn't hear him.

Lucky for him, it didn't look like he was helping me because of how hard I tried to throw him off me and go after Annabelle.

Then I was lost in the fight again, my fists crushing the bones of I didn't know whom. The rage finally left me empty and I snapped back into the reality of why I was there. The ring. And then I saw Dario climbing up the wall of rock. I warded off fists as I watched Serafino pulling himself up from the ground and climbing after Dario. The Archangel's stone clambered down and crashed into Serafino's face. He fell back with blood dripping down his face. It pooled at his feet as he climbed again.

The clang of metal against stone rang out as someone yanked my hair from behind. I spun around with gun at the ready. Drusilla stood there with blackened skin, her chewed up fingernails swiping at me. She looked like a demon straight out of hell. I shot the red-haired whore in the face. Lava sparked through her veins as she fell back and her jaw flew off her and crumbled to ash.

I looked back and there he was, ring in hand. Beneath him, Serafino tugged at the leg of his apostate subordinate. And Serafino, Dario, the lance, and the ring all fell to the ground.

With the thud of bodies against earth, the fighting ceased. We all stood there motionless, watching and waiting, knowing the following moments would define all our fates.

They grappled against each other and for the briefest of moments Dario's eyes met mine with a steadfast gaze—the most expressive look he ever gave. The Holy Lance flew from his hands, aimed right toward me. No one flinched or jumped to retrieve it. But in his second of distraction, Serafino knocked the ring from Dario's hand. They started after it on hands and knees, Dario rising to his feet with each step. I now held the lance in my hands. In the distance, an owl hooed once. Then twice. And with one last look at me, Dario drew his gun. His lips mouthed the words: 'keep your promise.' Then he aimed at the ring. And fired.

Chapter Twenty-One

AN EXPLOSION OF FIRE AND DUST billowed up and out. Thunderous. My ears rang and everything unfolded in slow motion. I was engulfed in shock. It was like a movie. But as quick as it came, it was gone. After it settled, I knew the dust of the explosion had been the ash of Awakened. The only ones who remained were Annabelle, Serafino, Gabriel, and I. Four had perished in the inferno. And now there were all those worn faces, in this worn out place.

Gabriel was dying before me. Serafino crouched next to him, and Annabelle stood beside me, licking blood from her lips with a venomous glamour. Her haunting yellow eyes gleamed with anticipation and she sauntered forward to Serafino.

He was a miserable sight to behold. One arm had been blown away, a leg was bent all the way backward, and a broken jaw clung to its last ligaments. One eye was now only a gaping hole with a tattered optic nerve dangling over his charred face. He was living, breathing roadkill. He bared his fangs at us, his one red eye all blood and malice. His one arm swung at me—his final attempt to intimidate looking just the opposite.

"Fucking leech."

The last words he ever heard.

Annabelle plunged her stake into his heart and he fell back, silent and comatose. I emptied my gun into him and with three shots he disappeared from existence without a trace. All ash to be washed away by the rolling tides of Lake Michigan.

I turned to Gabriel. Barely alive Gabriel. Black fog slithered away, but for this single minute, I didn't care.

"You'll kill me too?" he croaked.

Blood matted his hair to his face. Still beautiful, despite the damage inflicted by the fists and the fire.

"No," I said. I walked over to the place where Sage's ashes were still heaped. A sick heat swept through me at the sight of it. "If you die here, then you die," I threw the lance into the lake and picked up her machete. Under-neath it laid her ring. "But I sincerely want you to live."

I walked back to him with her ring in my hand. Bending over his broken body, those green eyes trembled as they looked into mine. An infinite paradox danced between us, where the only thing that was doubtlessly understood was love. I held his hand and slid the ring onto his finger.

"Twist it," I said, "and it will cloak you in shadow, fog, whatever you wish. Protect yourself. Heal."

"Will I see you again?"

"I hope so."

I stood up to leave, to hunt down Annabelle. Sage's machete was in my hand. My feet crunched against the stones as I walked away.

I stopped. Looked back at him. "You told me my eyes reminded me of someone you once met. Mornor. I never told you…. He's my Sire."

"Small world." The smallest smile lit up his face. "Goodbye, sweet Maaria," he said, his voice thick with emotion and blood.

"Goodbye, Gabriel."

And I turned and walked away. I don't know if he's alive or dead. Three decades and I've never seen him, never heard a single word about him.

I HADN'T SEEN WHICH WAY SHE'D GONE, BUT I knew where she would be, where I would find her.

When I reached the church, her black fog loomed front and center. She didn't want to run away, she wanted to put on a show. Violent hemorrhaging of my rage was imminent. It convulsed just beneath the surface, threatening to burst forth, but I wouldn't let it. I wouldn't give her the satisfaction.

Sage's machete hung by my side as I approached and Annabelle's fog vanished, revealing a twisted and bloody grin.

"Aren't you curious, Maaria?"

I didn't answer. Stopped walking. Twenty yards stood between us.

"How I knew about the Regency? The hunters? Where to find the ring? Don't you want to know?"

She knew better than to wait for a response.

"That girl. At the bar. I know you saw her," she said, with syllables climbing up and down dissonant scales. "When you met with that British bastard. She was there. In the park. My blood slave."

I responded by letting the blade swing dangerously in my hand.

"You stupid bitch," Annabelle taunted, "you think you can kill me?"

I said nothing. Only walked toward her. The machete was a swinging pendulum, distracting her as my other hand crept toward the gun in my pocket.

She laughed. A nervous quivering in it.

"The ring is gone. We've got nothing to fight over anymore. You're going to ki—"

A bullet to the chest interrupted her as she fell to the ground with fiery veins. I ran and sat on top of her, my knees digging into her arms, pinning her to the ground. I tossed the gun aside and took out my stake. It all felt so familiar; only this time it was real.

"Do it," she said stonily. "Kill me."

Her yellow eyes bore into mine, lachrymose and in agony, swimming with tears. When she spoke, her voice shook.

"Sometimes," she choked. "Sometimes I have dreams where I'm dying. They're the best dreams I could ever have. A few hours where I don't have to pretend anymore."

I thrust the machete toward her and held the tip against her throat. It sliced into her skin as she swallowed against it.

"Before you do it, Maaria…tell me one last thing. Make me feel good."

There was a moment of resounding silence and then the soft flapping of wings. An owl passed by, letting out a lone hoo. I looked up at it. That made seven. And she would be the seventh to die tonight.

"Aasurakasa," I said.

Her eyes met mine one last time and I drew the blade away from her neck, exchanging it for my stake.

"There will be no tomorrow."

She closed her eyes to never open them again as I shoved the stake right through her heart. I shoved myself off her and looked down at her torpid body as a single tear rolled down her face. I was standing next to the building that started it all. It was Annabelle and Sage in there that night. I knew now that it was. And my final words to Annabelle—before she would crumble to ash—would honor Sage. The first word I ever heard her say.

"Bitch."

And then I raised the machete and drove it through her neck.

Chapter Twenty-Two

T HERE MAY NOT HAVE BEEN A TOM-
orrow for seven, but there was for me. The
night after the end, I woke with a heavy heart.
I had lost everything. I first lost everything when my
mortality was taken from me, and in only a month I
had lost everything again. When I was Awakened it
didn't matter so much; I couldn't remember what I lost
so there was no burden to carry when I lost it. This
was different. I started with nothing and gained so
much—friends, a sister, love, humanity, a sense of
self—and now it was gone. Humanity and a sense of
self...these were things I wish were gone. They were
too heavy to bear, looming there with the weight of
eternity on my shoulders. An infinity of empty
promises.

I felt as if everything I had gone through,
everything I had lost had been for naught. What did it

matter if the Regency had gotten to the damn ring? Would it really have made any difference to me? How could my future look any different if we had won or lost? I'm doomed to the same curse at the end. I had watched members of my own race being cremated right before my eyes. And for what? What made me any more worthy to exist than them? Sure they might have been vile, but so am I by my very nature.

I had no more right to live and no less reason to die, to perish in my own personal inferno.

I am nothing more than a cadaverous abomination wandering aimlessly on this living sphere now. A dazzling sense of clarity, littered with undertones of death. Or perhaps more accurately, just death, reliving the clarity of life through blood. I am a psyche slipping into a vaguely remembered dream. A candid actor.

As I sat up on my mattress, I was just a single point of pale pink-white light. An intersection of distracted voices and cluttered silence. I was a sick pining; a longing with nothing to long for.

Even now, as I write this, I still feel it. Though it has lessened. I have found a beauty in this darkness and a darkness in the beauty of life. I have learned to become indifferent to everything in this life. In-difference—the subtle atrophy of the soul. But this is exactly what I needed. To become less human. Or at the very least, more detached. I truly began to listen to

Mornor's words—to take things with a spoonful of cynicism.

Erasing my humanity was never in becoming some animal like I initially thought. That was foolish. But I am far less human now than I have ever been. I still feel, am still tortured by these emotions and tides of humanity, but I am no longer afflicted by that thing which defines every human's life—that signature distress caused by the ticking of the clock. The ricochet of panicked questions, the right or wrong, the fear of death which controls every human decision whether they know it or not, and which controlled me for far too long after death, is finally gone. It has no more hold over me. I have already died and the thought of my final death no longer fazes me. I stopped caring about the events of the world around me, about how my actions would affect anyone else living or dead, stopped worrying about morality, about time, about pain. I embraced what I am for the first time. Because if this is what I am doomed or destined to be, then I will experience it in all its richness. I will experience it for what it is, not for what I want it to be.

But back to that day, back to that speck of pale light. Back to the day after the end.

A KNOCK AT THE DOOR. THREE KNOCKS. SOFT, but measured. My heart would have skipped a beat if it were still pumping; my thoughts conjured up visions of Gabriel standing out there, knocking on my door just as he had done at the bank. And instead of the eyeless butler answering the knock, it would be me. There could be a happy ending.

But this isn't a fairy tale and it wasn't Gabriel at the door. It was Barth. Standing in the doorway, face markedly weary, that thick charcoal moustache the defining feature.

"May I come in?"

His voice was grave and I stepped aside to let him in. I closed the door behind us and dropped back down onto my mattress. Our faces both shared the same expressionless look of defeat. He pulled up the desk chair and leaned back in it, much the same manner as Sage. It made me all the more anguished.

He let out a heavy sigh.

"I must thank you. I know what you lost last night and I have the deepest respect and gratitude for what you have done. What you have sacrificed. I know there is nothing I could do to ever repay you. This life will never be fair to any of us."

"Did I do a good thing? The right thing?"

He eyes drooped, making him look even more tired and enhancing that look of woe on his face. "It is what you make of it. For me, you did a wonderful thing. You freed me of my duties. For the Primus, wherever he may be now, you did a terrible thing. You robbed him of his power. For your friends who died, you did a beautiful thing. You carried out their mission to destroy the ring once and for all.

"You," he pointed at me, "you must decide for yourself if what you did was good in your eyes. You can choose for it to be your burden or your liberation. But it is your choice, and yours alone, to make."

My eyes welled with tears and my shoulders trembled, but I fought off the urge to shatter into a million tiny pieces.

"Don't fret, Maaria. You have an eternity to make that decision and to move on from it."

Not exactly comforting words. An eternity. A forever to live with this terrible loss, regret, and victory. I bowed my head and wrung my hands; like if I watched them carefully enough, I might be able to wring out the agony and glimpse it falling to the floor.

"Thank you," Barth whispered. "Every ounce of my being thanks you for what you did. No one will ever need to carry the burden of my duties again and I owe that all to you."

There was a pause. I looked up to see him with his eyes closed, his head rested against his hand. With a sharp exhale he looked up at me.

"But I must ask one more thing of you, Maaria. One last favor."

"What is it?"

"I dare not damn anyone else with this curse. So I must ask you—" He cut himself off and looked away, his body wincing in pain. "I must ask you to do the honors of gifting me with my final death."

If I said I hadn't been shocked, I would be lying. But after that initial shock, there was only the uncomfortable sensation of my stomach sinking. I didn't find this to be an honor—only another curse.

"You want to die?"

He nodded. "Yes."

"Are you sure?"

He almost chuckled. "I have never been more sure of anything, my dear. I am tired." He paused; took one final look around the room. "Do you wish to know how old I am?"

"Sure," I breathed.

"My mortal body died in 1433."

I tried to do the math.

"Nearly five hundred and eighty years, Maaria. I am ready to go."

I nodded. Cleared my throat. Another human gesture. But it felt fitting, as this was a human thing to do—take another man's life, to set him free. It took a deep mutual respect and connection.

"Okay," I said and took my stake from my pocket and Sage's machete from the floor beside my bed.

Barth slid from the chair and kneeled on the floor before me.

"I have to ask," I said with these murder weapons in hand. "There was a girl. She told me where I'd find the ring. She knew about the rock, the sigil, the box, the lance. Everything. …Who is she?"

A wistful smile graced his face. "Ah, I should have known. I met her years ago in New York, when I first came to this country as Reverend G. Christian Barth. She was an Old One like me, though I think she deserves to be called an Ancient One. She is the oldest vampire I have ever met. I told her about the ring. She was far too old to trifle with such things. Yet here she is," he smiled.

"I thought you couldn't tell anyone where the ring was?"

"That's the funny thing about her. I didn't need to say it aloud. She heard me anyway."

"Who is she?" I asked. "What's her name?"

"That is not for me to tell. If she wishes for you to know her name, then she will do so. But if you happen to see her again, tell her I say goodbye, will you."

"I will."

Our eyes connected and for a brief moment we were equals, as his existence hung in the balance between life and death. Existence and nothingness.

"Are you ready?" My voice shook.

He made the sign of the cross over his chest and muttered to himself, "Ashes to ashes, dust to dust. I will return to the ground from whence I was taken. For I am dust. And to dust...I shall return." He finished with a nod and closed his eyes.

"I am ready."

So I plunged the stake right through his heart. And before his body had time to topple over, I swung the machete and sliced through his neck. And he dissolved into a pile of ash at my feet.

I took some ash, decided keep it. I didn't know where I would learn the ritual to create my own Ring of Darkness, but I would be certain to find someone to teach me. And I would use his ash to do it. A reminder of the vampire whose mission took everything from me, but also the one who revealed to me the truth of unlife. The rest of him, I gathered up and scattered outside. There, he would return to the ground from whence he was taken.

And now everyone I had known was gone.

TWO DAYS LATER, AS I WAS PREPARING TO leave that town forever, I had another visitor. Not announced by a knock at the door, but with an overwhelming presence. I knew who it had to be. And when I opened the door, there she was in all her marble beauty and her luminous hair, the ragged old dress, and the naked feet. In her hands was a scrap of paper. She looked at me with those glass violet eyes and held it out to me.

"When everything is gone, go here."

She spoke quietly. Her crystalline voice masked by smoke.

Timid, I reached out and took the paper. My skin never touched hers, but I felt her power resonating on my fingertips like a pulsing wave.

"What do you mean...when everything is gone?"

"When the time is right, and it has happened—you will know."

"Barth—"

But she was gone. Vanished.

Somehow I knew she would still hear, so inside my head I whispered, 'Barth says goodbye.'

And I felt a ripple of acknowledgement. A sad smile within me. Imagination or not, I was certain she had heard me.

On the scrap she had given me was scratched a set of coordinates. I still don't know where they'll lead me, and I still don't know what will happen to send me there. But I folded it up and placed it in my pocket—where it's been ever since—grabbed my tiny bag of belongings, and walked out the door of the shed for the very last time.

I never looked back.

Chapter Twenty-Three

AFTER I HAD GONE AWAY IT SEEMED for a while that I had been chosen. That this strange series of events had called to me, or that I had been called to them; that this was destiny. A fate which chose me to orchestrate the events that led to the destruction of the Ring of Solomon. How else could everything have worked so perfectly?

Not that it was perfect in the sense that it was in any way favorable. I lost Ralph and Sage. I left Gabriel, the man I felt a peculiar love for, dying in the dirt. Awakened were obliterated. I killed Annabelle for a second time, even though the first was only an illusion. And what for? Nothing. I did it so the very man who brought it upon us could ask me to kill him as well. And for some strange woman to leave me with more questions than answers. No, it was not perfect in the sense that it was favorable. It was hell.

But it was perfect, because how could it so happen that it was the Nobilis Sanguis' leader who would hold a collection of ancient artifacts including Longinus' lance, that it was he who sought the ring, who gathered the members of the Regency—one of which who would betray his own coterie and help me. How could it so happen that it was Annabelle who suggested I go search the library of St. Catherine's church, where I would find the code Barth had left? It's funny how things work out. Ralph had said step one was to keep the ring away from the Regency and step two was to dissolve the rest of them. I took care of both those things in one fell swoop. It's unfortunate he never lived to see it happen. It really is funny how things work out. It all fit together like pieces of an intricate and impossible puzzle. Things shouldn't have played out the way they did.

And it was all these things that lead me to believe I was chosen. It was I, Maaria, picked from the midst because I was the only one destined to save us from the tyranny of the Royal Blood. But this was just my way of coping. I wasn't chosen. This was all just miraculous chaos. Disaster would strike either way. If the Regency had won, it would have meant vast destruction. But they didn't win. And there was still destruction. It was just quarantined to one little stretch of shore. Lake Michigan's rolling tides.

No, there was no meaning. There was no fate. But I had played a part, been an active force that helped shape my future and the future of all vampires. And that random chaos gave me freedom.

It's taken me years to see it, and thinking about my first month of vampirism still hurts, but I know now that without it, I likely wouldn't have survived this long.

Those days are past. They are gone. And I am still here. I have moved on. I have detached. I understand now that this existence is a giant and infinite oxymoron, and that I will never figure it out. I will never find what I am looking for. And just as Barth told me—it will always be unfair. But I have finally learned what Mornor meant when he told me to let go of my mortality.

And after it ended, the night the Ancient One left me with those questions which still have not been answered after these thirty long and lonely years, and after I left, walked out of the shed to never return, I listened to the wind. And on that night and on every night since, the wind has whispered to me:

'Maaria Naeva.

'Maaria, Born at Night.

'This.

'This is your second chance.'

COMING SOON…

BLOOD BATH

Read on for an exclusive preview…

Blood Bath

They say fame will go to your head. Well, when you're famous for one of the most gruesome strings of murders in modern history—and you let it get to your head—things can get a little carried away. I'd paint you a nice linguistic picture of the story, but the scene can tell the story all on its own. Walls splattered with fifty shades of red, viscera and assorted long-dead organs scattered across the floor. Silver torture-cages caked with layers of dried blood and a bathtub filled with it. You get the idea.

I am a murderer. But you can't blame me for it. It's not my fault. They broke the rules. They broke the most important rule. So what did you expect me to do? Sit back and watch? It was murder or be murdered.

We were the Bathorian Countesses. A feminist coven whose members praised and exalted the doings of Elizabeth Bathory—The Blood Countess, the

Bloody Lady, the Rejected Princess. And everything we did paid tribute to her. All our rules served to preserve her practice. And in the end, I think we paid her the highest of honors.

The mortals loved it, ate it right up. First H.H. Holmes in the north, now this is in the south. It was violent, it was salacious, it was Victorian Gothic, and visceral to an extreme. Five-star performance art. But to other vampires, this was a PSA: 'Ahem. Ahem. May I have your attention, please? At first this was just a bit of fun for us all. But yes, I admit it quickly got out of hand. You can now put your worries to rest. We leave this exhibit here so you may see that matters have been taken care of. The threat to our Midnight Masquerade is dead and gone. Please return to your normal, ordinary, blood-sucking unlives. Thank you, thank you. Take care. Goodbye.'

Mortals didn't know it was us right away. The murder spree. They didn't know until it ended. They missed out on all the fun. The Countesses really were something else. Without us, the vampiric underground would have been a little less Theodore Gericault in *Anatomical Pieces*, a little less Francisco Goya in *Saturn Devouring his Son*, and a little more Henry Fuseli in *The Nightmare*, a little more tame. So it's a shame it all had to come to an end. I'll miss that dedication bordering on recklessness. But...that's about all I'll miss. Aside from the jolly blood splattering, the Countesses were a little too high-strung and misanthropic for me. A little too Bouguereau in *Dante and Virgil in Hell*. Always degrading men, seducing them, forcing them into complacence for their own amusement, all so they could kill them and drink their precious, inferior blood. A little too classic horror movie for me—the sweet and innocent little girl who ends up being the killer. They always lived up to their stereotypes. So predictable. So boring.

So how did we get here? How did *I* get here? Not too long before this blood bath of a scene, I was a bright young girl with a promising future. I was attending one of the most prestigious all-girl boarding schools in the country in the magnificent Académie de Broussard home in New Orleans. The streets were full of rich culture and rich young boys all tipping their hats at the young ladies in the silk gowns and skirts and chemisettes. All this etiquette and modesty swirled together with the macabre and promiscuous; the freak shows and post-mortem photography, the phantasmagoria and burlesque. And I was swept up in the middle of it. So how did I get here, to this room full of body parts, blood, and ashes? How did I become just as famous as H.H. Holmes or Jack the Ripper?

To answer that terribly complicated question, we're going to have to start on a humid summer day in the streets of superstitious New Orleans, year 1888. I was seventeen, beautiful, innocent, and worshipped the modest traditions of the time. Things change, I suppose. Things change really really fast.

So please, come back there with me, walk the streets with me, feel the thrills with me. Prepare to taste the blood in your mouth, feel the blade in your hand, and get ready to witness the performance of a lifetime. Ready?

Let's go.

ABOUT THE AUTHOR

Nicki North is a writer, vampire connoisseur, and
Music Business graduate from small-town Wisconsin.
Born at Night is her first novel. Learn more at:

www.nickinorth.com